PEDALING WEST

A NOVEL BY
E. A. COE

PEDALING WEST
Copyright © 2023 by E. A. Coe

FIRST EDITION SOFTCOVER
ISBN: 1622533607
ISBN-13: 978-1-62253-360-2

Editor: Lane Diamond
Cover Artist: Kris Norris
Interior Designer: Lane Diamond

EVOLVED PUBLISHING™

www.EvolvedPub.com
Evolved Publishing LLC
Butler, Wisconsin, USA

Printed in Book Antiqua font.

Books By E. A. Coe

Pedaling West
The Road Not Taken
The Other Side of Good
Full Count

Author's Note

Thank you for reading *Pedaling West*. While the story is fictitious, and not really a bicycling story — more a literary suspense, and the story of a young woman's personal growth — bicycling serves as a backdrop against which the story unfolds, and the places and routes referenced are real. Over 2,300 rail-trails exist in the US today, including the Flint Hills Trail in Kansas. Close to 1,000 additional rail-trails are currently in stages of planning or development.

Together, this unique network connects our country's historic past with the future, providing opportunities for healthy exercise and safe bicycling. The trails have also become a source of increased tourism in the communities they serve, regenerating positive economic impact from the valuable infrastructure created for railroads in another era.

To learn more about rail-trails, I encourage you to contact the national non-profit Rails-to-Trails Conservancy (**www.railstotrails.org**). I'm especially excited about a rails-to-trails initiative occurring near my home. The 50-mile Shenandoah Rail Trail (**www.shenandoahrailtrail.org**) will connect my community with 10 others in the Shenandoah Valley when it is completed in 2030.

Thank you, not only for your interest in *Pedaling West*, but for your support of biking in America.

~ E. A. Coe

Prologue

The worldwide catastrophe that began in 2020, resulting from the COVID pandemic, exacted a frightening toll on human lives and created a global economic crisis of earth-shattering proportions. In March 2020, the United States government accelerated gargantuan programs to protect its people and businesses from disaster. By July 31, 2020, the Small Business Administration had received over 14 million COVID-19 Economic Injury Disaster Loans (EIDL) applications, of which it approved 3.2 million for $169.3 billion. During that period, the SBA disbursed 5.8 million emergency advance grants for $20 billion.

Quoting the Inspector General in a report released on October 28, 2020, "To expedite the process, SBA *lowered the guardrails* or relaxed internal controls, which significantly increased the risk of program fraud. The unprecedented demand for COVID-19 EIDLs and the equally unprecedented challenges to respond to pandemic issues, combined with lowered controls, resulted in billions of dollars in potentially fraudulent loans and loans to ineligible businesses."

By July, the Inspector-General had identified over seventy-five billion dollars of federal aid funds and grants to fraudulent applicants. That number continues to grow as ongoing investigations continue.

Chapter 1

"What! You're firing me?" Carrie forced herself to close her mouth behind the N95 mask, certain all color had drained from her face.

"I prefer to characterize it as laid off because of necessary downsizing," said Norman Sloan, founder and Chief Executive Officer of Pilgrim Burgers Llc. "After months of fighting the COVID-19 crisis, I can see the health emergency isn't going away soon. My priority to keep the company solvent forces me to make unpleasant decisions now."

Carrie Brinkley, Internet Technology Manager — at least until now — wasn't happy. "Put a bow and ribbon on it with pretty words if that makes you feel better. The result is the same. You still own a business, and I don't have a job."

"I'm sorry, Carrie. This meeting pains me greatly, but I have a fiduciary responsibility to place the firm's best interests ahead of my personal feelings."

"I understand, but my initiatives have much to do with our success through the first months of this emergency. The automated social media blasts I started doubled our takeout business, and I'm the one who figured out how to file for Payroll Protection Loans online. I see the same data as you and Teresa, and Pilgrim Burgers' net profit currently runs ahead of the same time last year."

"I'm aware, Carrie, and appreciative of your efforts this year and the past three. I doubt we'll change our computer systems much until the end of 2020, and maybe beyond, depending on the coronavirus. Maintaining a salaried position to manage that during this crisis isn't cost-effective."

"You could do many things to lessen the burden of my salary, short of firing me. I've performed every job in the company, including cooking on the line, so I'm having difficulty understanding your decision. Does this have anything to do with my questions about the COVID loan money?"

"Of course not. You comprehend the financial complexities of Pilgrim Burgers better than anyone besides Teresa and me, and I would expect you to want to understand our strategies for surviving the pandemic crises. Your curiosity about the deployment of the funds received through our COVID-19 loan initiatives has nothing to do with my decision. The draconian measures required to survive the pandemic necessitate trimming temporarily unnecessary management. Again, I'm sorry."

***

Carrie Brinkley had graduated near the top of her Business Information Technology class at Virginia Tech's Pamplin School of Business three years earlier, and turned down job offers from several prestigious consulting firms in favor of a unique opportunity near her hometown. The Pilgrim Burgers CEO and his Chief Financial Officer, Teresa Dill, had attended a Career Day event sponsored by the college, and the position they offered intrigued her.

Their small, Tidewater, Virginia-based company had grown from one unit to five in three years, and they sought talent to increase it even faster. The idea of joining an expanding franchise had appealed to Carrie, and she particularly liked Teresa Dill, a smart woman only a few years older than herself.

A whirlwind thirty-six months of rapid growth followed, in which Carrie played a key role. The company seemed poised for a potential initial public offering—until it slammed into the COVID-19 crisis.

She let those thoughts go.

The short meeting in Sloan's office had started one of the worst days of her life, which continued on her drive home. The flashing blue lights of the James City County patrol car behind her surprised Carrie, and she pulled to the shoulder of the road.

The police officer approached her car, and pointed to the expired inspection sticker on the windshield.

"What! You're ticketing me?" exclaimed Carrie.

When the officer explained that Carrie's vehicle inspection was nearly two months overdue, she accepted the citation, glumly placing it in the glove compartment. She couldn't imagine the day getting any worse.

But it did.

Trey Goodson's Porsche sat in the driveway when she arrived home. The starting right-fielder for the local Triple-A Tidewater Tides, Trey was also Carrie's lover. If Trey received the call-up to the major league club this summer, as most expected, Carrie suspected an engagement proposal might follow. Drafted in the second round by the Baltimore

Orioles, Trey had led their Norfolk minor league club in home runs the previous season, and enjoyed a brief visit to the majors when clubs expanded rosters at the end of the season.

Trey leaned against his car and smiled oddly at Carrie as she stepped out of her car.

"Hi, Trey," she said. "I'm glad you're here, because my day has been awful. Let's go inside."

Trey fidgeted uncomfortably with his car keys, remaining near the driver's side door. "I'm afraid I can't stay long, Carrie. I received some bad news this afternoon and came over to tell you about a decision I made. The big leagues officially canceled the minor league season today, and players will only receive a four-hundred-dollar monthly stipend to maintain contracts. When Baltimore drafted me, I lacked thirty-three credits to earn a degree in Finance from Alabama. I'm going home, and plan to take their online classes to graduate."

"What? You're breaking up with me?"

"Let me finish. I apologize for the short notice, but I'm leaving this evening. I have nothing else I can do up here, and the university will allow me to use their facilities for workouts. My parents own a large home there where I can live, and Alabama seems like the best place for me to ride out the pandemic. Hopefully, things will return to normal soon, and I can get back to baseball — and you."

At a loss for words to respond to such an egotistical, self-serving, and heartless speech, Carrie replied with three. "Good luck, Trey."

As he leaned in to hug her, she walked past him to her door. On the way, she noticed two bicyclists pedaling through the neighborhood. Under her breath, she whispered, "Can I please go with you?"

Inside her condominium, Carrie plopped on the sofa, tears welling towards an inevitable flood. Then she remembered one of her favorite childhood stories and chuckled. *Alexander and the Terrible, No Good, Very Bad Day*, by Judith Viorst, had, until now, established the definitive example of bad luck, either real or imagined. Now, having been terminated, ticketed, and jilted within the past two hours, Carrie thought she may have established a new benchmark.

The bike leaning against the wall near the front door beckoned, and she decided a long, strenuous ride might be good for her. As she considered all that had gone wrong the rest of the day, she pinched both tires before leaving, to make sure they weren't flat.

CHAPTER 2

"That's one," said Sloan, sliding into bed.

"The easy one," said Silky, still concerned about the whole mess. "Why did you fire Brinkley first?"

"Because she already questioned why we aren't using the COVID money to bring back employees. Both she and Dill can access the company's financial records, so does it make a difference who goes first?"

"I guess not, but you need to put some space between the terminations to keep the rumors down, and Dill appears more dangerous. She knows you inflated the payroll estimates to achieve higher Payroll Protection Program loans."

"Dill might be angry, but she won't say anything. All the loans went through with no questions."

Sylvia Brown, known to friends as "Silky," had worked for the CFO, Teresa Dill, for several years. As the Disbursements Manager, Silky accessed the financial records for the company regularly. Her job included making deposits and preparing expense checks.

Born to poverty on Church Street in Norfolk, Silky had earned an athletic scholarship for track at Norfolk State University. Determination and hard work led to regional hurdling championships during all four years of college, to accompany a Bachelor of Science degree in accounting.

She spent no time celebrating her graduation, though, despite being the first in her extended and eclectically related family to accomplish such academic achievement. The diploma represented another tool in her growing arsenal of weapons, and her ticket out of the inner city. With a drive for personal wealth and success in life that bordered on obsession, she remained unburdened by rules or boundaries to achieve either.

Silky's life also allowed for no time-consuming distractions such as vanity. With smooth ebony skin wrapping a shapely physique like a surgical glove, raven-like eyes, full lips, and hair professionally straightened semi-annually, she epitomized contemporary ethnic feminine beauty. However, she didn't make physical attractiveness a goal. Her body only presented another means for achieving objectives, no different from her intellect or ambition.

Far from a delicate flower to hold and behold, Silky contained the potential of a tightly coiled spring ready to explode powerfully and randomly. Her gifts facilitated a relentless pursuit, making her a dangerous adversary to anyone blocking her path. She learned early in life that neither gender nor race presented barriers, but rather traps for the gullible, and she used these to ritualistically defeat those who underestimated her.

These days, Silky pretended to *like* her boss, Teresa, and to *love* Teresa's boss, Norm Sloan.

Her younger brother, Damien, lived with her. He'd completed a shortened prison sentence at the Blandy Correctional Facility for participating in an armed robbery involving a weapon, and, after his release, Silky allowed him to stay at her Denbigh apartment. Though discharged early for good behavior, Damien was neither reformed nor good. He shared his sister's warped strategy for succeeding, but lacked her patience. Silky hoped his tenancy at Blandy might have tamed his impulsiveness.

The extra guest in her small apartment didn't inconvenience Silky, since she preferred Sloan's less crowded and more luxurious accommodations on the Elizabeth River. Her not-so-private relationship with him provided an elevated lifestyle, with the requirement to sleep with him only a nuisance. Besides that, Silky had targeted Sloan as a convenient opportunity.

He was twice married, and his former wives eventually tired of their roles as ornaments and toys, unaccompanied by respect. Both intelligent women had found it effortless to catch him cheating, which resulted in lucrative divorce settlements.

His current girlfriend had discovered that his unbounded ego and addiction to flattery, false or otherwise, made Sloan easy to manipulate. The extraordinary sum of money accumulating in his company because of COVID-19-related loans provided all the incentive Silky needed to maintain a relationship with the man.

Weeks earlier, she had suggested to him a plan for a more personally satisfying utilization of the funds.

***

2020 started innocuously, but then world news began reporting a strange virus affecting people from the Chinese city of Wuhan. Most United States citizens paid little attention to the information until the country's first victim showed up in the state of Washington on January 21. By January 23, Wuhan instituted strict quarantine measures, and on January

29, President Trump announced a task force to study the new flu. Two days later, on January 31, the World Health Organization declared a public health emergency. Three days after that, the United States did too.

The pandemic escalated worldwide in February. Various countries curtailed travel, most instituting strict isolation mandates. On February 26, President Trump announced his assignment of Vice President Michael Pence to manage all responsibilities relating to the health emergency in the United States.

Broadway went dark in New York City on March 12, the same day the NCAA canceled the storied March Madness college basketball tournament. The National Basketball League suspended all future games that day, and Major League Baseball's commissioner temporarily postponed the opening of the 2020 season.

Days later, Congress passed the historic Coronavirus Aid Relief and Economic Security Act (CARES), authorizing over two trillion dollars in federal funding. The comprehensive legislation strengthened existing federal relief programs and broadened others. Congress established the Payroll Protection Program (PPP) within the act, explicitly designed to help businesses continue to pay employees during the pandemic crisis, and it relaxed restrictions for firms to apply for Economic Injury Disaster Loans (EIDL).

Teresa Dill alertly followed the news of the government's plans for helping businesses, and created documents for COVID-19-related loan requests under the PPP and EIDL programs within days of CARES enactment. A quirk in how Sloan operated his string of fast-food businesses allowed Dill an opportunity to capitalize on the amounts requested for each loan.

Pilgrim Burgers comprised twenty-one separate, stand-alone, limited liability companies. The awkward organization caused complicated financial tracking and reporting for the company's CFO, but the strategy kept Sloan's individual companies small enough to avoid the requirements of the Affordable Cares Act. The ACA mandated that larger businesses offer health benefits to employees. Under the recently legislated CARES act, Pilgrim Burgers could apply for the maximum amounts allowed for each of the twenty-one units.

Dill's interpretation of the broadened provisions of the EIDL program resulted in applications for funding improvements at each unit, to facilitate takeout orders. She also applied for the maximum limits of PPP money, using guidelines provided in the legislation for average monthly payroll calculations.

Sloan had reviewed the documents his CFO prepared for the bank approvals, and revised them without telling her. When the loans resulted in higher amounts than expected, Dill alerted Sloan to the difference, and he admitted to inflating her estimates for payroll before sending the applications. Though outraged by her boss's audacious ethics violation, she felt helpless to do anything about it.

***

At the time, Sloan had devised no ambitious plans for COVID-related funds accumulating in his corporate accounts. The ease with which the loans transpired had surprised him, and the extra money provided a comfortable cushion for the company's operations during a difficult time for food-oriented businesses. Because of the practical measures his team took to reduce expenses while increasing takeout service, all twenty-one of the Pilgrim Burgers locations remained profitable. Sloan had no compelling need to spend the government money yet, and he resolved to keep all options open for how to utilize the extra funds.

Then, Silky gave him an idea.

As she lay naked next to Sloan one Saturday morning, Silky asked, "Norman, honey, what do you intend to do with the PPP and EIDL money in our cash accounts?"

"What do you mean?"

"It's a simple question. What part of it didn't you understand?" She glared at her bed partner, her dark eyes unblinking.

For a pregnant second, Sloan stared back. "Watch the attitude, woman. Your question confuses me because it's stupid. You know the reasons for those loans."

Silky sat up in the bed. "That's right, Norm, I do. I'm also aware we received twice as much PPP money as Teresa expected. You changed the figures in the loan requests she prepared without telling her, so I'm curious about your plan."

Sloan relaxed back on the pillow with his hands behind his head. "Did Teresa say something?"

"No, but I helped her accumulate the data she needed for the SBA documents. You doubled her estimate of each unit's average monthly payroll."

"So what?" retorted Sloan. "The SBA paperwork required a guess, and while the government provided sketchy guidelines for preparing it, they didn't consider every factor relating to all businesses. We've increased the company's size by sixty percent in the last two years, and could arguably grow it again this year. I added a cushion to Teresa's numbers to cover that potential."

"I don't need an explanation, and I don't care why you inflated the number. After receiving the PPP loans, we didn't increase our payroll or bring any employees back, and I see little development on the drive-through renovations. Since you aren't using the money for those things, where will you spend it?"

"Capital projects take time, and Teresa informs me the government allows two years to allocate the PPP funds. What's your point?"

Silky turned away from Sloan and exited the bed on the opposite side. Her bare body glistened against the morning sun pouring through the expansive windows.

Sloan groaned. As she pulled on tight-fitting jeans, he tried to salvage the day's start. "Come on, Silk, stop it. I'm trying to figure out what's on your mind. Why are you angry?"

As she fastened a lacy bra, she faced him from her side of the bed. "Because I don't appreciate men who treat me like some whore whose primary function is evening amusement! I'm a manager in your company, and thought we progressed past being only lovers. My mistake! Anybody with a brain can see what you're contemplating, but if you don't plan to include me, fine! Good luck, cuz you're gonna need it."

"Whoa! Hold on there! You're way ahead of me, because I don't know yet how I'm going to allocate the COVID funds. Yes, I inflated the request, and the cash sits in our banks, but I'm not in a hurry to spend it. As I understand the legislation, money not distributed on time converts to a low-interest loan, so I'm keeping the money available for a variety of contingencies. You *will* be a part of any strategy I create — when I create one."

Silky quit buttoning her blouse and sat on the edge of the bed. "OK. We could have avoided this disagreement if you had told me that the first time, but I'm still disappointed you have no clear idea how to use the funds. Let's talk about the money. Our balances show over nine million dollars spread over twenty-one different accounts. For starters, that amount of capital needs a better home."

"What are you suggesting?"

"That you and I could live the rest of our lives nicely on the level of wealth you presently control."

Sloan sat up and stared at his girlfriend. "You want me to steal it?"

"I don't like that term, but an opportunity to *appropriate* the money for better purposes seems available. How much did Eastern Equities expect you to make by taking the company public?"

"They didn't provide a hard number because it depends on many variables. My calculations project something in the ten-million-dollar range—on the high side."

"Right! Which comes after a lot of energy and good luck. Part of the payout would also depend on a lengthy earn-out, requiring you to work like a madman to keep the company's financials solid through the first several years after the public offering. You'll no longer have autonomous control of your company or your life because you'll serve a board of directors. How do you think a group like that might view an inter-company relationship like ours?"

"You make the IPO sound unpleasant, but it still beats prison. How would we pull off a fraud of the magnitude you're suggesting?"

"The biggest health crisis in history provides a monumental distraction for this country and our entire world. The government is desperately trying to stave off small business collapse, creating massive economic relief programs they don't have the resources to monitor or manage. You significantly exaggerated Teresa's estimate of our average monthly payroll to each bank providing our units PPP loans, but did anyone question it?"

"No," said Sloan. "I expected them to, but they didn't. If they had, I planned to explain that past payroll isn't an accurate tool to project future amounts for a growing company. Even if they disagreed, I figured they might only require me to re-submit the paperwork. Not a single bank questioned the estimate, which shocked me."

"Not me. Our banks had no incentive to look for reasons to disapprove loans to a financially secure business customer, because the government backs the loans. Upstream, the SBA's efforts to distribute the money preoccupies them so thoroughly that I doubt extra resources exist to audit the local loans that banks approve. The same sort of indifferent oversight resulted in the EIDL approvals for additions of drive-through windows at each of our units."

"What's wrong with those? Customers can no longer come *inside* restaurants to get food because of COVID restrictions, so adding better ways to pick it up *outside* seems justified."

"True, but the way I read the requirements for EIDL loans, the money is supposed to be used for operational expenses. Building *repairs* qualify as operational expenses, but characterizing upgrades to drive-through infrastructure as repairs is a stretch. It doesn't matter now, because the SBA approved it."

brief vacation between jobs, followed by a new career in a larger company. The position would compensate her well, and she would meet her future husband, becoming a wife and a mother. Her retirement in a spacious oceanfront cottage on the Outer Banks of North Carolina would be comfortable.

She, however, chose the other option, hitting the "send" button and closing the computer.

***

Silky waited for Sloan as he entered his house later that evening. "You have a problem, Norm."

Well, shit. "What now? I terminated Teresa this afternoon, so you and I remain the only ones who can access our financial transactions."

"Did you escort her from the building?"

"No. I told her to collect her personal things and depart. She did nothing to warrant being treated like a criminal."

"That's what I thought. So, Dill could have loaded up a flash drive with computer files or taken paper documents from the secure cabinets, right?"

Sloan slapped the coffee table and glared. "Why would she do that?"

"She didn't, Norman, because she didn't need to. She only had to send key files from her desktop to her home. I visited my new office this afternoon—where Dill used to work—and booted up the computer. Out of curiosity, I checked the emails my predecessor received recently and the ones she sent. Her last outgoing email, including three attached files, went to her personal Gmail address. One file listed the current balances in our investment accounts compared to the same balances in January. Another showed the payroll estimate she prepared for the PPP loans. The last looks like the form we sent the SBA after you adjusted it."

"Shit! Shit! Shit! What will she do with those?"

"Hard to say. Maybe try to blackmail you—or send copies to some government regulatory outfit. Who knows, but she didn't copy the files as mementos of pleasant memories. I doubt she's figured out what she'll do with them, but those documents present a problem—which means she's a problem."

"Not that much. She has a record of the COVID relief money in our bank accounts, and in the next two years, the government wants us to spend it wisely. Nothing requires using the funds immediately. We haven't done anything illegal—at least, not yet."

"Maybe, but you doubled her estimate for average monthly payroll to qualify for larger PPP loans...."

"I can explain my reasons for that, and if an auditor ever discovers the change, I doubt we'd be punished for an undefined administrative error."

His answer clearly didn't satisfy Silky.

"This presumes the relief money accumulated will remain where we can distribute it" she said, "or return it to the government. That isn't our plan, but it will have to be if Teresa Dill raises suspicions with regulators. She stole financial records that can make you appear guilty — which is a bad sign."

"So, what do you propose?"

"I'm not ready to give away nine million dollars yet. I'll take care of this."

"Like how?" asked Sloan.

"Like... you shouldn't ask so many questions, Norm."

"I don't get why you believe this is so important. The files Dill took with her don't prove squat. Nothing she took can hurt us much."

"Wrong, Norm! What if she calls a bank regulator, or somebody from the SBA, and tells them she thinks you're trying to embezzle COVID-19 relief money?"

"Then whoever investigates our accounts would find all the loan money still there. If we accidentally submitted defective paperwork, so what? We'll correct it, and sorry about that."

"Exactly! *Sorry about that* — so take the money back. No harm, no foul, right?"

Sloan sensed his next words would be wrong even before he said them. "Right, and nobody's in trouble."

Silky's eyes smoldered, unnerving and dangerous. "And nobody's rich. You would ensure everything with the COVID money went squeaky clean from here on out if you thought anybody suspected you of a crime."

"To avoid a prison sentence? Of course."

"My point, Norman. We're close to a considerable payoff — and we don't have to risk jail. We need to keep a lid on our strategy for a couple of months. If Dill is suspicious, she still knows next to nothing. She could, however, guess enough to sound an alarm that would derail our plan. I've gotten comfortable with my vision for our future, baby. Let me handle this."

Sloan wanted to resist, but Silky's leg rubbing against his now made logical thinking difficult for him. "OK, I guess," he mumbled as she pushed him down to the couch.

After finishing the call, Carrie felt satisfied she had fulfilled an obligation to a former business friend, but irritated she committed to looking at purloined Pilgrim Burgers documents. One goal for her planned trip included leaving everything to do with her former company behind, and now she would carry smelly little reminders with her as files on a travel laptop.

She heard the notification of Teresa's email arriving at her desktop computer, and quickly transferred the attached files to an empty folder. Before leaving, she would move the folder to a USB drive to take with her. She then deleted the email from Teresa as an afterthought, once she stored the files on the desktop.

The doorbell rang, and Carrie guessed it would be her mother and father returning her bike. After setting Carrie up with a maintenance course on bicycle repairs with a friend who owned the bicycle shop in Williamsburg, her dad had urged her to leave the bike at the shop for a few upgrades. Since declining his suggestion didn't appear to be an option, she'd accepted the offer, and caught a ride home with her dad.

Carrie owned a Piker model bike made by the Shenandoah Bicycle Manufacturing Company based in Edinburg, Virginia. Founded by two young biking enthusiasts in 2005, SBMC was still relatively small, but the company's four production model bicycles enjoyed solid reputations. The Piker, named for The Old Valley Pike that traversed Virginia's Shenandoah County from north to south, featured durability and versatility, competing well with similar models from well-known manufacturers like Trek and Surly.

It had been at the shop for four days, and she couldn't guess what sorts of upgrades might take that long to accomplish.

Her mother came through the door first, giving Carrie a cryptic signal with her eyes while glancing back at Hal.

Carrie didn't understand the sign until she saw the bicycle Hal rolled into her foyer. "Oh my God, Dad! Is this still my bike? I hardly recognize it!"

Hal beamed. "Yep! My friend reinforced all the bike's metal joints with a lightweight compound and swapped out both axles for heavier-duty ones. He also replaced the tires, brakes, and chain."

"Wow. Thank you, Dad." Carrie admired the bicycle. "What's this on the frame below the handlebars?"

"I had fun with that. I welded an aluminum cage to hold a Garman Edge GPS and an integrated SunVu minicomputer. The two reflectors on the front are small solar panels that should keep the unit fully charged, but four double-A batteries supply backup power. You can sync an iPhone to make or receive calls without using your hands. The computer also displays video from the wireless camera under your seat to let you check traffic approaching from behind. Everything can be voice-activated."

"I'm amazed, Dad! Where did you find all this stuff? I haven't seen anything like it on a bike before."

"Not sure anything like it exists. I bought the components online, and my friend assembled everything in his workshop. You only need to put the necessary information into the controller and then sync your phone. I put the instructions for the other features on this flash drive."

"What other features?"

Her mom rolled her eyes, and her dad hesitated but finally said, "Well, honey, your mom and I worry about your safety on a trip like this, so I programmed the controller with things that might come in handy during emergencies. For example, you gave us your intended route, so I matched each zip code you will pass through with the corresponding nearest police dispatch station. Wherever you are, when you give the command, 911, the system will connect you to the closest enforcement facility, either state or local."

Carrie hugged her parents. "Thank you, Mom and Dad, but I'll be fine. The course at Charlottesville made me aware of the dangers, and I plan to exercise all reasonable precautions. Please don't spend the next three months worrying. Some parties I attended at college might have been more dangerous than this trip."

"And you don't think we worried about you then, too?" asked Hal.

Her parents suggested taking her for dinner to the nearby Ruby Tuesday, which offered outdoor seating during the COVID-19 crisis, and she gladly accepted. With her refrigerator and pantry empty, a good restaurant meal sounded preferable to the takeout pizza she had planned. If they dined early, she would have plenty of time to finish packing when she returned.

***

Hal ordered a beer before the meal, as did his daughter, and Maddie asked for a glass of white wine. As they relaxed with drinks, Hal studied Carrie, who laughed at something Maddie said. After reconciling the fears about his daughter's quest, he now felt only admiration for her commitment. The bold and reckless endeavor seemed out of character for Carrie, but it touched something familiar in his subconsciousness.

Festival Marketplace, where the ferry vessel docked on the Norfolk side. The complex featured several fine restaurants and a variety of retail shops. Museums, boat tours, and other entertainment-oriented attractions were within easy walking distance along the waterfront, including Harbor Park, the baseball stadium completed in 1993. Carrie had spent many evenings watching Trey perform there over the last year. Today, however, she traveled not *to* this familiar place but *away* from it.

Alone with her thoughts as the boat carried her to Portsmouth, her pulse quickened. The mild exercise of the past two hours didn't cause it, so she wondered if the elevated heart rate resulted from excitement or the first signs of panic. She willed her mind to review the pertinent data she accumulated before deciding on the adventure.

She might ride alone, but she would encounter many other bikers on her journey. Over forty-seven million citizens enjoy this form of recreational activity every year in the United States, and the pandemic pushed even more significant numbers into safe outdoor activities, like biking and camping. However, few would attempt a coast-to-coast bike trip, and of those, most would not travel solo. Carrie preferred to complete her unique mission alone. Was that naïve?

The mild jolt from the ferry touching the dock interrupted her thoughts, and Carrie walked her bicycle down the gangway.

Later in the afternoon, she stopped in Holland, Virginia, located west of Suffolk. A Subway meal purchased next door lay next to her on the hotel bed as she checked her iPhone. She responded to a text message from her parents, then opened her small laptop to review the route for the next day. At that moment, she realized she had not copied the Pilgrim Burgers files Teresa sent her from her home computer to the travel laptop. After checking her iPhone, she also remembered deleting the Gmail containing the documents.

Damn!

She wrestled her conscience for fifteen minutes, deciding not to call Teresa. Carrie wanted no responsibility for whatever files Teresa might have taken and desired no further involvement with Sloan or Pilgrim Burgers. She understood her friend's disappointment—make that irrational anger—but believed Teresa should move past it and get on with life. So, why hadn't Carrie just said that in the first telephone conversation rather than agreeing to study the files?

There it was, though. Carrie had committed to reviewing the documents, and "reliability" counted as one of her admirable traits in life. She hoped she might find, or build, some equally good new traits on this epic bike adventure but decided she shouldn't discard already established old ones. Reluctantly, she pulled up Teresa's name on her phone's contact list.

Nobody answered, and the call went to a voicemail message. *Hello. This is Teresa, and I'm not available now. I'll return your call at the first opportunity, so please leave a detailed message.*

"Hi, Teresa. Carrie Brinkley. I started my bicycle trip today and forgot to transfer the files you sent from my desktop to my travel computer. Unfortunately, I deleted the email after downloading the documents, so I can't re-access it from my iPhone or laptop. Could you email them to me again or call me back? Sorry for the inconvenience."

After leaving the message, Carrie mentally placed a check in the box for fulfilling a personal obligation. She was glad Teresa hadn't answered the phone, but experienced a tinge of guilt for hoping her friend might not even return the call.

***

"Nice job, Damien." Silky handed him an envelope. "There's ten grand in there, and you'll earn more if our plan works. Keep your mouth shut, and don't go showin' off the money!"

"I have more experience at this end of the business than you do, Sis. I don't need instructions."

"Sorry, I know. So, what do you think about the files on Brinkley's computer?"

Damien thought for a few seconds before answering. "I don't think we can fix that problem by throwing another computer in the river."

"Why not?"

"So far, we've left no evidence connecting what happened to Dill back to her former company. She just disappeared. The theft of a computer owned by another employee occurring around the same time Dill went missing could create a link. That's a long shot, but I don't think we should take the risk."

"So, what's the alternative?" asked Silky.

"Do you know where Brinkley lives?"

"Yeah, she's single and has an apartment in Newport News."

"Well, she ain't at home because she just started a cross-country bike trip. I could break into her place easily enough."

"Even if you could, I'm sure she protects her computer with a password. She's one of those IT geeks, so she's probably careful about security."

"I'd be shocked if she wasn't, but Deshaun down on Granby — you've met him, Aunt Estelle's kid — has a computer shop. He's always accessing hard drives for rich folk. The computers get locked up, and sometimes the people who own 'em can't remember the password they used to protect 'em. Deshaun gets into the hard drive without the password and restores the files to a different drive. The people with the problem can then download their stuff to a new computer. If I can get Brinkley's computer, Deshaun can access anything on it."

Silky smiled as she thought. "No harm in tryin'. Brinkley won't return to her apartment for a coupla' months. Knowin' her, though, she's got her door and windows hooked up to an alarm system."

"Shit, Sister! Most of the people out in Chesopian Colony did, too. Never held me up much."

CHAPTER 7

When Silky informed Sloan she had evidence that Teresa Dill sent the incriminating stolen files to Carrie Brinkley, his face lost color, and he slumped into the seat behind his desk. "Are you sure?"

"Am I sure she sent files? Yes. Am I sure they were the same ones she took when she left? I can't tell yet, but I can't think why she would send different ones. Am I sure Brinkley received them? According to her voicemail, Brinkley needed Dill to resend them. I don't know if that means the files didn't go through or Brinkley lost them. Wherever they are, we need to find them."

"How did you access Dill's phone?"

"Do you really want to know, Norman? You can trust that I did."

"No, I believe you, but let's think about this. Those documents mean nothing if we clean up our act here. We can start processing contracts to build the drive-through windows at all units, and if anyone inquires why we're late getting started, we'll blame it on the chaos of the pandemic. Dill might have suspected I contemplated fraud based on the documents I doctored for the SBA loans, but she's the one who told me we didn't have to use the PPP money right away. She had no proof of anything, so I'm not all that concerned about what she might have sent Brinkley."

"Not so fast, Sloan." Silky sent a clear and intimidating message by using her boss's last name. "You have a partner to consider in this deal now, and I'm not ready to give up nine million dollars that easily. Our bookkeeping may appear sloppy if we ever get audited, and maybe we sent the wrong numbers by accident to the SBA when we estimated our payroll. That's no reason to start directing the money we have to what the government wants versus what we want. Dill's gone, and we aren't certain Brinkley even received the files Dill sent her. If she did, she might do nothing with them. Brinkley and those files create a liability, but I see no reason to panic."

Sloan's face flushed red, and perspiration appeared at his temples. "You aren't my partner in anything but occasional intercourse, and that part of our relationship won't put me in jail. Your family has a more either side of the road featured spacious homes commanding panoramic vistas. Smaller homes and single-wide trailers, often resting in the shade of giant satellite dishes, populated the lower elevations.

From out of nowhere, the Bland Correctional Center came into view ahead of her to the left. An uninformed passerby might mistake the well-manicured facility for a college campus, but the tall chain-link fences ringed with barbed wire surrounding the buildings established the complex's more ominous purpose. The secure enclosure provided comfort to those who passed, but Carrie still found herself pumping faster to ride by it.

CHAPTER 8

When Carrie called her parents from Bluefield, her dad asked if she had heard about Teresa Dill.

"No. What about her? She called me the day before I left Virginia Beach, and sent me something I forgot to download to my travel laptop. I called her later to resend the files, but my call went to voicemail. She hasn't returned that call."

"The *Virginian Pilot* had a brief article on Monday," said her mother. "The newspaper reports she went missing early this week. Her parents became worried when she didn't answer their calls, and they went to her condo on Sunday. Her car remained parked on the street, but Teresa wasn't home. They had a key and reported to police that nothing in the condo seemed disturbed. Their daughter hadn't told them of any travel plans, though. Newport News Police issued a Missing Persons Report."

"Shit—sorry, Mom—I mean, crap! Teresa was a friend at Pilgrim Burgers, and now I feel bad about not wanting to take her calls after I started the bike trip. I can't imagine the things we discussed have anything to do with her missing, but it makes me wonder—and worry."

Carrie completed the call, providing her parents with a detailed update on her trip, but her mind remained distracted by her concern for Teresa.

She set her cell phone aside and typed a code into her microcomputer to access the Pilgrim Burger's mainframe. The hack she effectively executed was illegal, but she blamed Sloan for doing nothing to update his IT infrastructure password codes after terminating her. Since she had been the one to create the algorithms for daily password changes, she could correctly determine the current day's code by looking at a calendar.

She rationalized that the crime she now committed was justified. She wasn't just vicariously snooping around confidential corporate records, but attempting to discover a connection between company files and a missing person. She noticed few changes since she'd last surveyed the records as a legitimate manager. No new PPP or EIDL funds appeared, and the company had spent none of the initial funding. She exited the accounts, then did a google search for "government fraud tip hotline."

CHAPTER 10

As Damien broke into Carrie Brinkley's place, for reasons he couldn't pinpoint, thoughts of his four years of a scheduled ten-year sentence at Bland nagged at the back of his mind.

Damien matched his older sister in intellect and a complete lack of ethics, but unlike Silky, he acted impulsively. While she applied brains, appearance, and education toward longer-term criminal goals, he preferred more immediate results. His recklessness had netted him a sentence for accessory to armed robbery, which he'd accepted stoically. He performed as a model prisoner, earning early parole for good behavior.

Nobody who knew Damien believed his time at Bland had reformed him. His tenure at the prison, among the facility's more seasoned and knowledgeable residents, provided him with advanced skills that made him a more dangerous criminal. His Ph.D. in "bad" now complemented Silky's diligence, creating a lucrative opportunity for both of them. Damien appreciated her willingness to allow him to help.

Accessing Carrie's second-floor condominium proved easy, since the building maintained no security and the stairwell doors were unlocked. The Amazon delivery uniform he wore turned out to be a superfluous prop, as he saw nobody inside the condo complex.

He slipped on surgical gloves to pick the front door lock, entered the residence, and closed the door behind him. The condo featured six rooms, and Carrie used the extra bedroom as an office. He booted her desktop computer to life and, as expected, the system required a password, so he turned it off.

He checked the desk drawers for other storage drives and found none. The trashcan next to the computer tower on the floor was empty, and only a large Atlas map occupied the desk's surface. Damien unplugged the desktop tower and placed it, along with the map, inside the bag he'd brought.

For increased safety, Damien sprayed the computer screen and all the surfaces around the desk with a cleaning solvent, wiping them thoroughly with a soft cloth. He did the same at the doorknobs before leaving, and exited the building using the back stairwell. Because of COVID-19, people stayed indoors, and Damien saw nobody in or around the condo during his entire visit.

***

When Silky entered her apartment two days later, Damien's demeanor portended positive news. "Deshaun transferred the contents of the hard drive to a USB, and as I predicted, she kept her entire itinerary on a folder on the desktop."

"Do you still have the computer?"

"No, it's back in her condo, but I put the file on your iPad."

"What about the files Dill sent Brinkley? Did Deshaun find them?"

"Yep, the folder holding the documents was also on the computer's desktop. I put all three files on the iPad."

"Great! Are the files still on her computer too?"

"No!" said Damien. "I'm not stupid. I deleted the folder, but there's still no way of knowing for sure if the files are on Brinkley's travel laptop."

"But in her voicemail to Dill, she said she forgot to transfer them."

"Right, but Dill attached the documents to an email. That email isn't associated with a particular computer. It's stored someplace in the Google Cloud, and anyone with the right password can access it. Unless someone deleted it and cleaned the Gmail trash bin, the original email remains."

"Shit! I hadn't thought about that. Did you see any emails on the home desktop?"

"No, that would require having passwords for Google. Deshaun didn't think he could access emails stored on the computer without her Gmail security information."

"OK. No problem. Do you think we can locate Brinkley using the itinerary she created?"

Damien produced a lined notebook. "Her route divides into one-day legs with evening stops, normally at Super Eight or Days Inn motels. She designates accommodations along her route with red or blue dots, depending on the motel available. The miles she can accomplish each day likely determine where she stops for the night, but the map pinpoints the locations of the preferred economy motels."

"OK, but if she doesn't make reservations, how can you tell where she'll be?"

each day. She slept well and woke with little or no aching from the previous day's activity.

She recognized the need to increase daily caloric intake to accommodate the more rigorous athletic level. The usual dietary routine of juice and a bagel in the morning, followed by a sandwich for lunch and a salad with light dinner, no longer sustained her adequately. She now packed almonds, protein bars, and a banana into one pannier each morning, and added an electrolyte supplement to the two water bottles.

Most economy motels she selected for her journey didn't offer breakfast options, so Carrie developed a habit of shopping for dinner and the following day's breakfast and lunch simultaneously at the end of each biking leg. Grocery stores near her motel room represented the preferred choice for shopping, but sometimes simple convenience stores or 7-11s sufficed.

Breakfast usually consisted of boxed cereal, yogurt, milk, and a pastry, while lunch included two prepared cold sandwiches, a bag of chips, fruit, a health shake, and a packaged dessert. Beans and rice burritos or wraps became a favorite lunch when she could find them.

Most restaurants remained closed for inside dining because of COVID-19 restrictions, but a few provided takeout service. When overnight accommodations ended up close to one of these, Carrie treated herself to a full hot dinner she took back to her room.

If a full-service dining business didn't operate near her motel, Carrie found ways to create complete dinners from the stores nearby. Rotisserie chicken with fresh vegetables and two rolls from the bakery proved a consistently popular meal if a Walmart or Food Lion was convenient. Delivered pizza provided another alternative, and sometimes she rewarded herself with two cold beers.

Carrie washed her small load of clothes every third day using coin-operated washers and dryers, and she recharged her cell phone and microcomputer each evening. Before departing in the morning, she packed ice into the insulated part of her pannier and filled both water bottles from the bathroom sink.

Her computer provided a way to read books at night, but Carrie spent most of her free time researching the next day's bicycle leg before sleep. Google Maps' comprehensive satellite imagery allowed Carrie to review her planned route virtually, sometimes causing her to re-route a segment. She began pedaling each morning already familiar with the studied route's challenges and landmarks.

***

Damien ordered detailed printed road maps for Kentucky, Illinois, Missouri, and Kansas from Amazon. By analyzing the itinerary Carrie had created on her home computer, he estimated she now biked between Middleboro and Elizabethtown in Kentucky. He began working backward from Elizabethtown, calling economy motels in the communities Carrie selected for overnight stops.

If he could narrow her location within the area Carrie now traveled, he could find her using a vehicle. His only potential problem would be if Carrie altered her planned itinerary after she started. A Super 8 existed in Elizabethtown, but the clerk answering Damien's call said no guest named Brinkley had stayed there. He doubted Carrie made it beyond Elizabethtown, so he tried motels in towns on Carrie's route ahead of that one.

None of the motels in Springfield, Kentucky, had any record of a past guest named Brinkley. In Berea, front desk receptionists at two economy lodging businesses reported the same.

Damien began to wonder if Brinkley used a fake name to register for overnight accommodations, but then he got lucky with a clerk in London, Kentucky. After expressing an urgency to reach Brinkley because of a family emergency, Damien convinced an employee at the Minitel Motel to check her register for the past week.

"Yes, sir," said the clerk. "A guest by that name stayed here two nights ago for one evening. I'm afraid that's all the information I have. Will that help you?"

"Yes, thank you," said Damien. "This is most useful, and her family will be appreciative."

Damien exhaled in relief and looked at Carrie's itinerary. She'd reach Elizabethtown this evening if she kept to her schedule; by doubling her goal for the day, she might make Tell City, Indiana. Damien waited until ten o'clock in the evening to try the Super 8 in Elizabethtown again. If Carrie didn't have a room there, he would call the only other budget motel near the town, the Knights Inn.

"Super 8 Motel. My name is Yvonne. How may I help you?"

"Hi, Yvonne, I'm trying to reach a guest named Carrie Brinkley."

"Hold, please," said the clerk.

"Hello," answered Carrie.

"Oh, sorry. I think I reached the wrong party," said Damien, at once disconnecting, irritated the front desk clerk had given him no warning collaboration with the heads of several other organizations, facilitates an annual schedule of special training programs for selected agents, designed to enhance the collective understanding of our respective missions, personnel, and capabilities. Your name came up to attend one of these next month."

"I've heard about those sessions, and I'm flattered. Thank you. If you're allowed to tell me, how did my name come up?"

"I brought it up. I know some folks going, as well as the main topic for weekend discussions. Agents from Homeland Security, the DEA, and ICE will attend. I'm going, and my friend Randy Warren, Special Agent in Charge of the Cincinnati Field Office, will as well. Have you met Randy?"

"No, I didn't get more than a hundred miles away from Baltimore while assigned in Maryland. Where will the meeting be?"

"You'll like this, Doug. It's at the Greenbrier Resort, about a hundred fifty miles south of here. We'll have rooms at the resort, but the meetings will take place in the old bunker on the grounds. You can't get more private than that."

"I've read about that place, but thought congress decommissioned it back in the nineties after a newspaper reporter exposed its existence."

"That's exactly what happened, but resort employees still maintain the plumbing, electrical, and HVAC systems. The government started constructing the facility during the Eisenhower administration to provide a safe place for members of Congress to continue to conduct business in the event of a nuclear attack from Russia."

"So now the resort books it for meetings?"

"Not really. They sell tickets to tourists who want to see the bunker but don't schedule it for banquets or events. The Greenbrier's ownership are fans of the bureau, though, and they accommodate us when they can. We need to arrive on the evening of July 10, and we'll head home on Sunday afternoon, the 12th."

"Thank you, Jim. Sounds like an interesting weekend."

Hill looked forward to his personal tour of the legendary bunker. He also felt certain his supervisor knew more about the reason for his selection to attend meetings in it than he had revealed.

CHAPTER 13

Neat and fetching Berea, Kentucky, charmed Carrie. Forty miles south of Lexington, off Interstate 75, the town lay in gently undulating geography between the elevations of Dead Horse Knob and Welsh Mountain. The principal attraction since 1855 here was Berea College, and the community's pride in its coexistence with the legendary institution manifested itself on nearly every street.

Founded as the South's first interracial and coeducational college by famed abolitionist Reverend John G. Fee, Berea required no tuition from students. Instead, the college encouraged each to learn a craft such as woodworking, basket weaving, pottery, or glassmaking, and students sold their unique products at shops scattered throughout the town.

After settling into her room and checking messages on the iPhone, Carrie remounted her bike to explore. She had grown up cherishing her visits to the outlet malls around Williamsburg, but the merchandise in the Berea stores was different.

The shelves here displayed articles handmade by artisans who worked, lived, or studied within twenty miles of where she stood. As she traveled leisurely from one shop to the next, the shopping experience both stimulated and frustrated her. She discovered dozens of one-of-a-kind articles that would fit nicely in her condominium or make distinctive gifts for friends and family, but she only had her bicycle to carry them.

As she admired a beautifully carved sculpture of a knife and fork designed to hold napkins, someone behind her said, "We can ship those if you'd like."

Startled out of her reverie, Carrie responded, "Oh my goodness! I didn't see you there, but you must have read my mind."

"Not exactly," said the young lady through her mask. "I saw you park your bicycle in front of the shop. Those pannier bags attached to the back of it make me suspect you're on an extended biking journey."

"Very observant, and you are correct. Do you go to school here?"

"Yes, ma'am, but we're out for the summer. I'll graduate next year."

Carrie re-engaged in the bike leg she'd started earlier, threw the keys to the truck into the woods along her way, and biked to the police station in Tell City. A polite clerk led her into the police chief's office, where she downloaded pictures from her phone and her bike monitor.

Captain Pierce listened to her summary and reviewed the documentation. "We know these two, Ms. Brinkley. They're a couple of lowlifes who cause problems on the Kentucky side. They aren't in our jurisdiction unless we can elevate this to a federal crime. We can't do much."

"I thought that could be the case," said Carrie. "I understand."

"But, ma'am, I need to warn you about something."

"OK."

"Not only are Jug Harmon and Gene Stickling dangerous, but Harmon has a big family comprising of mostly criminals in Kentucky. To avoid additional risk, keep north of the Kentucky line and stay alert for the next few days. Try to avoid roads with sparse traffic."

"That sounds like excellent advice, sir, and I'll check my maps this evening. Am I safe in Tell City for the night?"

"Yes," said Pierce. "I doubt the Harmons would risk crossing the state line, but if you let me know where you'll stay this evening, I'll make sure a patrol car cruises by occasionally."

"Thank you so much, sir. I'm sorry to cause you this problem, but I appreciate your hospitality. I have a reservation at the Knights Inn at the edge of town."

"No problem, ma'am. If you see or hear anything unusual, call 911. We can get to the motel in minutes."

CHAPTER 14

From Tell City to Evanston is a straight shot on State Route 66. It disappointed Carrie to learn that this road had nothing to do with the legendary Route 66, which once traversed from Chicago to California. Unlike the country roads through Kentucky that eventually landed her in Tell City, the one to Evanston passed through modestly populated areas and featured light vehicular traffic. The route roughly followed the state line between Kentucky and Indiana, delineated by the Ohio River.

Outside of Hatfield, Indiana, traffic ahead of her slowed to a stop, and a large sign on the side of the road warned, "MEN WORKING." As she edged around Department of Transportation vehicles, several men with shovels worked in a sizable trench at the highway's edge, validating the road sign's alert.

A female wearing a yellow protective vest and matching hard hat, blond hair falling to her shoulders from beneath the helmet, supervised the men from the seat of a tractor with a bucket attachment.

Carrie smiled at the lady as she went past, giving her a thumbs up and wondering why cars hadn't been warned that *women* might *also* be working. Politically correct and inclusive caution signs most likely didn't rank high on the list of Indiana's priorities.

***

After pleasant evenings in Evanston, Indiana, West Frankfort, Illinois, and Steelesville, Illinois, Carrie anxiously anticipated the next day's ride to cross the Mississippi. She and her bike would take a tiny vehicular ferry leaving the Illinois side near Modoc and arriving on the Missouri side in historic Saint Genevieve. She judged the Mississippi River to be the one-third point of her journey, and she would complete that stretch in eighteen days, a day less than the schedule she created in Williamsburg. She understood, however, that the eastern portion of her journey consisted of much easier riding conditions than the western part would.

"And we've agreed he doesn't miss much," said Hill with a chuckle. "Thanks, Jim."

"That isn't why I stopped in. I'm driving down to the Greenbrier on Thursday, the day before the seminars start. The Bureau will pick up the extra evening of accommodations if you want to come with me."

"Thanks for the offer, but can I tell you tomorrow? There's a chance I might want to stay at the resort another evening after the meetings, so I planned to drive myself."

"No problem. Do you have friends down that way?"

"No, but someone might meet me there on Sunday if it's OK. That would be on my account, of course, and I'll need a day of vacation on Monday if things work out."

"Absolutely. I don't think you've taken a day off since you got here, and you come in on many Saturdays and Sundays. Take all the time you want."

"Thanks. The plans aren't final, so I may still go down with you on Thursday."

"Got it. Just let me know by Wednesday."

Hill glanced at the clock on the wall near his desk: 10:30, which meant Captain Mendoza would be at work. He took a deep breath, then dialed a Baltimore number.

"Special Agent Douglas Hill," said the female voice. "I worried you lost my contact information."

"No, nothing like that, Henri. I didn't have much to tell you, but something came up this week, and I wanted to run an idea by you."

"I'm listening."

***

Captain Henrietta Mendoza worked in the Southwestern District of the Baltimore Police Department's Operations Division. Two years prior, as a Sergeant Patrol Officer, she arrested Special Agent Hill at gunpoint for driving under the influence. The incident began the worst day of Hill's life, and the memory still caused nightmares. A drinking habit naively formed in college grew during Hill's first years as a successful and celebrated junior agent. After work, a few beers expanded to a half bottle of bourbon per evening, and sneaked shots of vodka became a norm at lunch.

Nobody except his concerned wife recognized the problem until too late. As he viewed the news on TV from his recliner one night, an emergency bulletin showed live coverage of a hostage situation occurring blocks away from the couple's residence. Determined to assist, he jumped from his chair, ignoring his wife's warning to stop.

He arrived in his vehicle near the crime scene and found three Baltimore police cruisers blocking traffic. Hill tried to steer through the blockade but missed, crashing into the back of a police car. Still obsessed with reaching the scene of the hostilities, he backed away from the damaged cruiser and attempted to redirect his vehicle. A young patrol officer stopped him by stepping in front of the car, her gun drawn.

"Stop!" she yelled. "Put your hands on the wheel, and don't move!"

In that awful moment, Hill sobered, recognizing what he had done and the extent of his addiction. The officer, whose nametag read "Mendoza," advanced to the open window, her gun still pointed at him.

"I'm FBI with credentials in my coat pocket," said Hill. "I was trying to maneuver around the blockade to the crime scene to help."

"Stop talking, sir," she replied. "Right now, I only see a drunk who shouldn't be driving. Is that a weapon strapped under your left arm?"

"Yes, ma'am. I'm permitted to carry it. Do you—"

"I told you to be quiet." She reached inside the car to remove the Glock 19 from its holster, and Hill caught the sweet scent of jasmine—mixed with fear—hiking his sense of guilt.

The police officer handed Hill's gun to another officer and holstered her pistol. After retrieving his credentials from his coat pocket, she told Hill he could relax his hands from the steering wheel.

As she examined the identification, Hill again tried to smooth things out. "I'm really sorry, ma'am."

She returned his FBI creds. "Not as sorry as I am, Special Agent Hill. I'll pretend you weren't trying to leave the scene of an accident, but any traffic incident involving property damage requires the driver to submit to a blood test. You need to step from your car and wait for me on that bench under the streetlight."

Hill observed the officer confer with her partners before she walked back in his direction. "My shift here ends in about fifteen minutes, so I volunteered to take you downtown for the blood test. You *should* go in handcuffs, but we'll forego that. Somebody at headquarters may also want you to stay overnight, but I'll do my best to convince them it isn't necessary. I'll give you a ride home afterward."

"Thank you, Sergeant Mendoza. I don't deserve your accommodations, but I'm appreciative."

Carrie had risen early from the Knights Inn in Harrisonville, eager to reach the entrance to the Flint Hills Trail. After reaching the trail, she planned to finish three hours biking on it before stopping in Ottawa for the evening. The discovery of the unusual biking path during her research had delighted her, but the trail wasn't paved. She hoped to test the speed she might achieve today on a short stretch to judge how long the entire length would take.

The community's name at the trailhead seemed familiar, but she couldn't place why — until she googled it.

Of course!

Osawatomie had become famous one other time in the nation's history, when John Brown and his sons lived there. The failed plans of the famed abolitionist and his group at Harpers Ferry had put the small Kansas community on the map in 1859.

Now, as she pumped her legs on the mostly deserted John Brown Highway, she marveled at the rural and inconspicuous geography compared to its fiery place in history. The flat land allowed her to see miles ahead of her, and she had not seen another vehicle on the roadway all morning. When one finally showed up on the handlebar camera approaching from behind, she could tell it traveled at high speed. She edged her bike well to the right of her lane for safety, suspecting with as little traffic as it carried, the road attracted infrequent enforcement.

***

Damien drove his vehicle near the single bike rider, increasing speed as he closed the distance. This deserted road presented nearly perfect conditions for his intended crime, and he resolved not to waste it. Placing a cell phone to his ear as a ruse, he brought the Jeep even with the bicycle.

***

As the car passed close to her left, Carrie briefly glimpsed the driver on a mobile phone. Then, suddenly, the vehicle swerved toward her bike. She reacted quickly, but not in time to avoid a collision.

She and her bicycle left the road into the gravel, and she flew ahead of it, headfirst toward the bank. Her body's forward momentum propelled her into a fence post, where everything went dark.

***

Damien stopped his car about twenty yards away, and opened the door to survey the accident results. He hoped Carrie's collision with the fence post had broken her neck, but he would if it hadn't. He'd acquired that skill in prison.

He walked only a few feet before a pickup truck appeared, coming from the opposite direction, still a half-mile away.

Damn!

He returned to the Jeep and drove the other way. Then he stopped. Doubting the pickup driver would have seen his car from that distance, he turned around and headed back toward the accident scene.

Damien hoped the pickup might continue down the highway without noticing Carrie or her damaged bike.

The truck, however, had stopped in the middle of the road, and the driver-side door remained open. A man attended to the prone body of the biker sprawled on the bank.

***

Russ Dennison spotted the disabled bicycle and slowed his truck. When he saw a body slumped near the fence line, he stopped on the highway and scrambled to where the woman lay. She didn't move, but Russ could tell she was breathing. As he pulled off his t-shirt to cover a wound on the woman's forehead, a Jeep drove past, going the other direction. Russ shook his head in disbelief that the car failed to assist, then reached for his cell phone to call 911.

"Don't move her," said the dispatch operator who took his call. "We'll send the ambulance and be there in ten minutes. If she regains consciousness before we arrive, try to keep her still. Did you witness the accident or notice other vehicles?"

"I didn't see the accident but noticed one car pass, going the other way. Other than that, nothing."

"OK. The ambulance is on the way. Hang tight."

The seconds dragged, and Russ checked his watch several times, but he could do nothing for the young woman until the ambulance arrived. He lifted the t-shirt from the woman's forehead briefly, relieved to see the bleeding had stopped. The cut didn't appear nearly as large as he initially feared. After several long minutes, a distant siren rose on the wind.

The red emergency vehicle screeched to a halt at the accident site, and Russ stepped back to allow emergency personnel clear access to the victim. As the EMTs removed the young woman from the roadside bank on a stretcher, keeping her head and neck secured, Russ marveled at their efficiency. The time from when the back doors opened after the ambulance arrived, to when they closed with their patient aboard, lasted less than seven minutes. Then the vehicle headed back in the direction from which it came.

***

Carrie regained consciousness and opened her eyes, and the sensation of movement alarmed her. She jerked against the restraining straps of what she finally determined to be a gurney.

"What's going on?" she said. "Where am I?"

"It's OK, ma'am," said the female EMT near the stretcher. "You had an accident, and you're in an ambulance heading to the Ransom Health Hospital in Ottawa. We should arrive in five minutes. How do you feel?"

"A little queasy. Also dizzy, and my wrist hurts. Did someone get my bike?"

"Yes. Russ Dennison, who found you, put your bicycle in the back of his truck, and he's following us. Nausea and dizziness are normal after a concussion. You may have a broken wrist, and a cut on your forehead will require stitches."

"Thank you. Was Mr. Dennison the driver who hit me?"

"No, ma'am. We aren't sure how the accident occurred and hoped you could tell us. Only Russ stopped, and he didn't witness the collision. Do you remember what happened?"

"Not much. Just that a car swerved into me as it passed."

"OK, that's a start. We'll pull into the emergency room entrance in a few moments, so relax. Once you're inside and comfortable, a deputy will want to talk to you about what you recall."

Carrie found the EMT's suggestion to relax difficult amid the efficient flurry of activity that occurred when she rolled through the doors. Two EMTs, nurses, and a physician helped lift her from the ambulance's stretcher to a hospital gurney. As one nurse pushed her into an examination room, the other slapped a cuff on Carrie's arm to check her blood pressure.

When she reached the curtained cubicle, the nurse who had pushed the gurney began cutting Carrie's shorts and jersey away with scissors. The other nurse inserted an IV into her left wrist. The nurse responsible for expeditiously undressing Carrie placed a light sheet over her before the doctor approached with a small light and a magnifying lens extending from his glasses.

"Still feeling queasy?" he asked.

"A big headache has replaced nausea," said Carrie. "Would it be possible to get a drink of water?"

"The headache is understandable, considering the bump beneath the cut on your forehead. I'm afraid a drink won't be possible until we check a few things, but that shouldn't take too long. Do you have any neck pain?"

"No. The pain stops at my forehead and starts again at my wrist."

"Good, good," said the doctor. "Will you move your toes and fingers for me?"

She complied, and asked, "How long was I out?"

"Well, we can't tell because we aren't certain when the accident occurred, but my guess is no more than fifteen minutes. The helmet saved your life, but you bumped your forehead pretty hard after hitting the fence post." The doctor alternated the small light from one of Carrie's eyes to the other as he spoke, using the magnifying glass to observe the result. "Your pupils dilate as they should, which is a good sign."

"Good. So, I'm going to be OK?"

"We're going to do our best to make sure of that, but we're just getting started. The reaction of pupils to light stimulation can sometimes help us determine the severity of a concussion, but a CT scan will show us much more. We'll also take some blood, stitch your forehead, examine your urine, and x-ray the wrist."

"Thank you, Doctor. I guess that means I might be here a while?"

"You've had a serious accident, ma'am, and I believe you were lucky. The fact you are talking and cognizant is encouraging, but head trauma like the one you sustained is serious. The negative effects are sometimes delayed and can be lethal. You'll be with us at least forty-eight hours, if everything from the tests turns out perfectly — longer than that if they don't."

"I feel a little lucky, all things considered. Thank you. And my name is Carrie, not ma'am."

"Great, Carrie. I'm Doctor Sam Long, and we'll try to make your accommodations here as comfortable as possible. Our food isn't too bad, and our rooms offer free internet."

The physician's wit amused her, and she smiled. "Thanks, Dr. Long. Will you be the one conducting the other tests?"

"Most of them, and I'll be here until after the wrist X-ray. Is there someone you would like us to call?"

"Would it be possible for me to contact my parents? I'd rather give them the news personally, and am afraid a call from the hospital would panic them."

"Certainly. If that can wait until after the cat scan, we'll retrieve your cell phone from your personal belongings. We'll also have you in a room by then, versus this cubicle. You'll have a little more privacy."

***

When the technician completed x-rays in radiology, a nurse rolled Carrie to a room. By this time, she was thinking clearly but worried that her headache and wrist pain were worse.

Within moments of being transferred from the gurney to a bed, Dr. Long appeared.

"Hello, Doctor. I'm glad to see you because both my head and wrist are hurting more than when I arrived at the hospital. Is that normal?"

"It is, Carrie, and we started some medication in your IV that should make you more comfortable shortly. The wrist x-ray shows no fractures, so your pain is from a likely sprain. The cat scans of your head and neck are also normal except for mild swelling underneath the bump on your forehead. The less positive news is that you have hematuria."

"What does that mean?"

"A moderate amount of blood exists in your urine. Since you aren't having a period, that could mean an internal injury. It could also result from something as simple as a bruised kidney. This evening, we'll run you through an MRI to check everything in that area. In the meantime, we'll wrap your wrist to stabilize the joint, and stitch the cut on your forehead."

"Thank you, Doctor Long."

"You're welcome, Carrie. If you feel up to it, one of our clerical assistants would like to get some information from you to complete your check-in to the hospital. Would that be OK?"

"Certainly, Doctor."

A couple minutes later, an administrative employee entered the room with a clipboard in one hand and Carrie's cell phone in the other. "The doctor said you wanted to call your parents, so I'll return with this paperwork when you complete the call, if that would be all right."

"That would be fine, ma'am, but I'm probably going to need some things that were in my jersey pocket. The nurses cut away my clothes when I arrived at the emergency room."

"No problem. We have all those in a box at the nurse's station. I'll bring them when I return."

Carrie's conversation with her parents was no better and no worse than expected. Her dad immediately reacted, and began sourcing airline reservations to Kansas City as Carrie finished the conversation with her mom, who agreed to call Carrie after they landed the following day.

When Carrie disconnected, the hospital clerk returned with the destroyed jersey that had been removed earlier. Carrie retrieved her driver's license and insurance card from the shirt's zippered pocket and handed them to the employee. "I no longer work for the company listed on the card, but believe my coverage continues through COBRA."

"We'll check that, ma'am. I'm sure you're correct, but when did your employment with this business end?"

"About two months ago."

"Good. COBRA benefits last for eighteen months, so you should be fine."

After the administrative employee completed the admissions record, Dr. Long and a nurse came back to Carrie's room. This time, they brought a needle and thread.

"How about if we take care of your forehead now, Carrie?" asked Dr. Long.

"Only if you promise I can have something to eat after that. I'm starving!"

The doctor glanced at the nurse and chuckled. "Sorry, Carrie, but as a precaution, we need to hold off solid food until tomorrow morning. You may drink, though, and we'll give you some medicine to ease the hunger."

"Shoot! Wish I'd have eaten a bigger breakfast this morning. Will you still be here after the MRI?"

"No. My shift ended thirty minutes ago, but I wanted to stay long enough to stitch your forehead."

"Thank you, Dr. Long! Remind me always to have my accidents in towns like this one."

"No big deal. I'm sorry your trip stalled in Ottawa, but I'm glad your accident was close enough to us to help. Were you able to talk to your parents?"

"Yes, they'll be here in the morning."

"I'll look forward to meeting them. I'll be back here tomorrow at two o'clock. Dr. Olson will check with you this evening with the results of the MRI."

***

The soft tap on the door woke Carrie from a light sleep, and she noticed the female physician standing at the door. "I'm Dr. Sophia Olson, Ms. Brinkley, and I have the results from your MRI. May I come in?"

"Certainly, Dr. Olson. I must have fallen asleep. Please come in."

"From what I read in the charts, you've had quite a day, so you deserve some sleep. I won't be long, though. Everything looks fine on the MRI. A bruised kidney causes a pinkish tinge in your urine, which will clear in a few days. How's the headache?"

"I still feel some pressure behind my eyes, but no pain from a headache."

"That's good. We'll continue to monitor that swelling another day or two, but I think you'll be fine."

"Thank you. Will there be any problem with bike riding?"

"Other than sore muscles, normal physical activity shouldn't present a problem once you're released. Your bicycle might be a different story, though."

"Oh, my gosh! I forgot all about the bike. Where is it now?"

"I have a note that Dr. Long left with me. The man who discovered you along the road, a Mr. Dennison, has your bike. He says it's damaged, and he gave us his contact information so that you can call him at your convenience. He left the two pannier bags attached to the bike with us, in case they contained things you might need here. We have those at the nurse's station."

"Thank you, Dr. Olson. I'll call him in the morning. If possible, I would like to get my phone charger from one of the panniers."

"Certainly, Ms. Brinkley. I'll have Nurse Denise bring both bags to your room."

CHAPTER 17

"I'm afraid the guy who stopped at the accident might remember my car," said Damien. "Also, the Jeep has a scratch on the right front door where it hit the bike. I shouldn't hang around here too long."

"What was Brinkley's condition?" asked Silky.

"I couldn't tell. She lay next to a fence post, not moving, but that's all I saw as I drove past. An ambulance arrived about six or seven minutes later, and they took her to Ransom Health Hospital here in Ottawa. She's alive, but I don't know her state beyond that."

"OK. We tried, but she's Sloan's problem now. Drive to Kansas City and catch the first flight you can back to Norfolk. Don't worry about the cost or how many connections — just get back here. By the time you arrive, I'll have reservations for us to fly someplace else. I'm pulling the plug here in Virginia, and have already lined up the banking, the visas, and an itinerary. We won't risk everything we gained so far for one last loose end, and I feel confident I can convince Sloan to clean that one up for us."

"What about the Jeep?"

"Leave it at the airport. We won't need a car until we land in Cuba."

***

Sloan accepted the call from the unknown number, confounded to hear the familiar voice on the other end. "Hello, Norm. I'm guessing you aren't having such a good day."

"Where are you, Silky?" demanded Sloan. "I tried to access the E-Trade account and can't. Did you change the password?"

"Um... yes, I did, Norm. I'm the administrator, and I updated the security details for the account yesterday. Doesn't matter, though, because it's empty. I transferred the funds to a safer place."

"What? You can't do that! That money belongs to the company, and I didn't give you authority to make transfers without my approval!"

"Sorry, but you're mistaken. I set up the E-Trade account in the name of S&B Investments, and the two corporate officers for S&B are you and

CHAPTER 18

Carrie slept restfully at the hospital, except for the interruptions every two hours for nurses to check the various monitors attached to her body. After she awoke, her favorite nurse, Denise, informed her that doctors had cleared her for solid food, and she ate a gigantic breakfast.

A deputy sheriff waited patiently outside the room until an employee removed the empty breakfast containers from the tray attached to the bed. When Denise introduced the officer, he said, "I'm hoping you may tell us a little more about the accident yesterday."

"I don't recall much. The vehicle was an SUV, a Jeep, and going fast. I saw the driver—a black male—and noticed he had a cell phone to his ear as the vehicle started to pass me. Suddenly, the car swerved, and the next thing I remember is the ambulance ride."

"Well, that is helpful because it corroborates evidence Russ Dennison gave us. After discovering you lying near the bank, he observed a Jeep pass by the accident site, traveling in the opposite direction. He hoped the car might stop to help him, but it kept moving. He also thought the driver of the vehicle was black."

"So, what does that mean?"

"We're not sure, but we think the Jeep Dennison spotted most likely hit you. The driver might have been returning to the scene to assist, but he kept going when he saw someone else there. He knew he caused the accident and your injury, so he may have wanted to avoid the insurance complications."

"Is that a crime?"

"Yes. Hit-and-run. With an injury involved, the violation becomes a felony."

"So, you're looking for the driver?"

"Yes. We posted an APB for a late model Jeep traveling in our area yesterday. Several fit that generic description, so we'll need more information to narrow the choices. Can you remember anything about the license plate?"

"No," Carrie answered, then hesitated. "Wait a minute! I do remember. The license didn't make an impression on me—because I've seen one like it every day of my life. I'm from Virginia, and it was a Virginia plate. I don't recall any of the numbers or letters."

"That helps. Jeeps with Virginia tags traveling around here yesterday reduces the search significantly. Would anyone from your home state have a reason to follow you here?"

"Are you asking if someone from where I live would try to involve me in a fatal accident?"

"I'm sorry, ma'am, and I don't want to scare you or jump to an extreme conclusion, but we consider all possibilities."

A distant shadow of a thought crossed her mind before Carrie answered. "No, I don't think so."

"OK. Good. I appreciate your help. We'll continue our search for the vehicle and its driver. Contact us if you think of anything else."

"I will, Deputy. Thank you."

***

Carrie waited in her room after lunch, dressed in a fresh hospital gown. When her parents arrived, her mom burst into tears at the sight of her daughter, and her dad quietly put his arms around Carrie, waiting for the right time to ask his many questions. Her mom had secured overnight reservations for two rooms at the local Holiday Inn Express, but they couldn't check-in before three o'clock.

"Well," said Carrie, "you'll only need one room tonight because my reservation here is for at least another day. The doctor wants to ensure that the swelling in the brain has fully subsided before releasing me."

"And then what?" asked her dad.

"You mean after I'm released?"

"Yes, what happens after that?"

"The doctor last evening said I should be fine for riding again. She thought I might have some sore muscles, but nothing that would preclude normal physical activity. My bike apparently has more than sore muscles, though. I have to call the man who has it this morning to get it back, and find out the extent of the damages."

Her dad ignored the news about the bicycle. "Carrie, you gave this a heroic try, but I hope you're planning to return to Virginia with us. You had a narrow escape, and I don't care about the damn bike. We'll get you a new one when we get home."

CHAPTER 19

At FBI's CJIS division in West Virginia, Special Agent Douglas Hill reviewed a flash alert in his morning communications traffic. CJIS maintained a massive data collection service that collated details about ongoing cases, recent criminal activity, and related information from tips, newspapers, and social media postings.

A sophisticated network of artificial intelligence applications continuously mined the database for unusual connections relating to unresolved cases. Law enforcement officials could request automatic notifications whenever someone logged new data about affairs of interest.

The memo Hill held matched the name of a person who had provided a recent tip to the Missing Persons Hotline in Virginia with the identity of a woman injured in a biking accident in Kansas. Carrie Brinkley supplied the information about Teresa Dill a month ago, and now she lay as a patient in Ransom Health Hospital in Ottawa, Kansas. He pulled the folder containing Brinkley's report from the wire rack on his desk, where, a few weeks earlier, he had placed it on a whim.

The connection between the injury and the tip seemed unrelated, but local authorities in Kansas believed the vehicle involved in the hit-and-run had Virginia tags. For Hill, the odds that a car from Virginia might travel a rural road in Kansas and randomly collide with a single bike rider from the car's home state defied reasonable plausibility.

His earlier premonition to keep the file handy seemed suddenly justified, and he suspected the random circumstances leading to the young woman's current lodging at a hospital in Kansas may not have been so random. Hill asked his administrative assistant to connect him to someone at the Ransom Health Hospital in Ottawa.

"Yes, sir," said the receptionist at Ransom Health. "Ms. Brinkley is a patient. Would you like to speak to her?"

"Yes, ma'am. Thank you."

***

Carrie answered the phone thinking she was rather popular today. "This is Carrie."

"Hi, Ms. Brinkley. Special Agent Doug Hill with the FBI's Criminal Justice Information Services Division speaking. Do you have a minute to talk to me?"

"Yes, sir, but what is this about?"

"Well, ma'am, I understand a motor vehicle hit your bicycle yesterday, causing an accident. We logged a report you recently provided to a Virginia Missing Persons Hotline, and our database system flagged the connection between your name and the incident. Are you OK?"

"I'm impressed, and thank you. Yes, I'm OK. I sustained a concussion, a bruised kidney, and a sprained wrist, but I'm hopeful the hospital might release me later today. Do you think my missing person tip relates to the accident?"

"Nothing substantial confirms that, ma'am, but the circumstances are unusual. I'm reviewing a report that states the vehicle that collided with you displayed Virginia tags. Is that correct?"

"Yes, sir, the front plate on the Jeep was the yellow 'Don't Tread On Me' kind. The collision happened too fast for me to notice a number."

"Right. I doubt you see many Virginia tags as you bike that part of the country. Are you concerned the accident may relate to the information provided to the hotline?"

"Until now, no." *But I'm sure getting a bad feeling.* "Should I be?"

"Not necessarily, ma'am, and I don't mean to alarm you. We have no additional clues relating to Teresa Dill, and no reason to investigate anyone at your former company. We become anxious when someone trying to help us with an unsolved case inexplicably becomes injured in an unusual mishap."

"I'm glad you can track that kind of random occurrence, and I appreciate you checking on me."

"You're welcome, ma'am. I hope you'll stay alert for the rest of the journey. Your incident was probably an unfortunate coincidence, but I would like you to keep my personal contact information handy. You may reach me at this number anytime, so don't hesitate to use it."

"Thank you, Agent Hill." After pressing the red 'end call' button on her iPhone, Carrie decided her conversation with the federal agent was not one she should share with her parents.

***

An interesting cross section of enforcement agency attendees had listened to stimulating sessions presented in the secure confines of the bunker. Earned or not, the FBI languished under a poor reputation for playing well with other regulatory organizations, so to participate in such high-level and secretive meetings with members of the ICE and DEA seemed unusual.

And civilians! Hill remembered the astonishing presentation by the minister, Tom Burns. Through his work with an international children's ministry, Pastor Burns had become a subject matter expert in human trafficking, but his detailed comprehension of underworld activities suggested associations that went far beyond his work with children. Sanchez and Harbison had attended the same lecture and, at different times, queried Hill about his impression of it.

On the first day of the meetings, Harbison had taken a seat across from Hill during lunch. Ostensibly, her selection had been random, but then she'd been more curious about his personal background than he'd expected. She affected a breezy conversational style throughout the meal break, but Hill had run enough interrogations of his own to know when he was the subject of one.

She chanced to meet him again the following morning as he doctored his coffee at the condiments station. This time, she mentioned her acquaintance with Johnson Bowie, the Director of the Fayette Juvenile Center. *"Small world,"* she'd said.

Sanchez had played at the same table as Hill during the after-hours Hold 'Em Poker tournament held on the first evening at the resort. Most who participated in this event displayed reasonable gambling skills, but not Sanchez. Since the competition required a buy-in of real cash, Hill wondered why someone so inexperienced would enter. He lost his stack of chips quickly, but took the early finish good-naturedly, purchasing a round of beer for the rest of the players. Hill, of course, declined the gesture, and Sanchez reminded him no rules existed about consumption of alcohol after hours. Hill found the brief conversation afterward awkward.

"I don't drink."

"Ever?"

"Never again."

"Is there an interesting story behind that?"

"Maybe. Not now, though."

When Sanchez had stared a moment too long, Hill broke the drama by dealing the next hand.

Was the other agent testing me? And if he was, did I pass or fail?

The chirp from his cell phone ended the reverie.

***

After the morning flight from Norfolk, Sloan rented a car from Hertz at the Kansas City Airport and headed to Ottawa. The suburb was less than an hour away from the airport, and Sloan suspected Carrie was still a patient at the Ransom Health Hospital located there.

He had checked with the facility the previous evening, and medical personnel would provide no information about her condition, but they verified Brinkley's occupancy. He considered contacting her parents but decided against it. Since he had no legitimate reason for knowing about Carrie's accident, a call might raise suspicions. He resolved to stay as patient and as invisible as possible for now.

Sloan understood that his strategy in Kansas hinged on the extent of Carrie's injuries. With significant wounds, she might not leave the hospital alive, in which case Sloan's concerns ended. If she survived her injuries but required extended convalescence, she would most likely return to Tidewater after leaving Ransom Health. She would only re-engage in the biking journey if injuries were minimal. Under that scenario, the medical facility might release Carrie before he arrived, so he kept the bicycle itinerary Silky provided him as a backup to locate her.

His primary purpose for the trip was to stall Silky from taking action that would immediately jeopardize him. With his negligible criminal experience, he had neither the desire nor the qualifications to successfully execute a murder on his own. However, if that became his only option to avoid incarceration, he would determine a way to accomplish it.

The Flint Hills Trail presented an almost optimal opportunity for Sloan's purposes if she continued her trip. He couldn't follow her in a vehicle on the trail, but the route featured many traffic crossings. Also, several communities along the way appeared to be nearly deserted. Finding a remote area to manufacture an unfortunate accident looked easy on paper. Until he knew about Carrie's medical condition, however, additional planning seemed pointless.

***

Carrie's parents helped prepare her for the short trip from her hospital bed to the hospital's front doors. She had on a new sundress and sandals her mom purchased the day before, and her dad held her two

"Which I have now resolved."

"Don't you want mine?"

Russ pulled his iPhone from a pocket, tapped the screen, and turned it toward her. "Is this it?"

"How did you get that?"

"You left it on the work order for your bike, and Jeff allowed me to copy it. I hope you won't sue him."

"No, I'm thinking of thanking him."

"We're on the same page then."

"Apparently, but you know I won't be in Ottawa long. I'm committed to my bike trip and need to finish it."

"I understand, but we can still enjoy the next few days. What time is dinner tonight?"

"My parents are taking me to a place they heard about that offers outdoor dining—Smoked Creations. Are you inviting yourself?"

"I have an idea your parents would like me to come. I know your dad would."

Carrie stared at the confident man in front of her, wondering if he was extremely perceptive or just forward. "You might be right. What do you think about baseball?"

"Hate the game."

"Me too."

***

A block away, Sloan lowered his binoculars as the couple entered the pickup.

***

The following morning, Carrie received a call from Jeff at the bike shop.

"I hope this isn't bad news," said Carrie.

"No, don't think so," said Jeff. "We started working on your bike but had to order a part that should arrive tomorrow. We have an idea we'd like to run by you and your dad if you might have some time today or tomorrow, though."

"OK, we can come down to the shop after lunch if that works."

She called Russ to have him pick her up for the ride on the trail at the bike shop versus the motel.

***

Carrie and her dad arrived at Ottawa Bike & Trail at one, and met Jeff at the counter.

Jeff wasted no time. "We ordered a handlebar to replace the damaged one, and we'll receive it tomorrow. We were able to straighten the fork, and we suggest changing out the chain and the tires while we have the bike here."

"That sounds fine. So, you might finish with the bike tomorrow?"

"Yes, or early Friday at the latest. We wanted to talk to you, though, because you made some interesting changes to your Piker, and we'd like your permission to make similar modifications on other Piker model bikes we sell."

Carrie glanced at her dad. "I don't think that's a problem, but I'll let my father answer. He sourced all the parts and put them together for me."

"You can get everything I added off the internet," her dad said. "Nothing is proprietary, so I have no patents or exclusive rights. I'm flattered you like them, and don't mind if you duplicate the accessories on other bikes. I can make the work easier for you by providing details of where I purchased the different components."

"That's nice of you, Mr. Brinkley, but you underestimate what you did. You created a distinctive bicycle, which we believe would appeal to other safety-conscious enthusiasts, through your innovative combination of existing technologies. We do a fair amount for Piker, including proprietary machining of parts for several of their models. We own another workshop south of town for that sort of engineering. The Piker Corporation could be interested in creating a limited-edition brand that incorporates some accessories you retrofitted on your daughter's bike. Piker couldn't register new patents on individual components previously protected, but they can trademark unique processes, incorporating patented parts used in new ways. Would you permit us to approach Piker executives with the idea?"

"Wow, Jeff, you understand bikes and your industry better than I do," her dad said. "Of course, you can."

"Great! If our discussions with Piker are productive, we'll work out the details of a deal. What would you think of naming the brand The Brinkley?"

Her dad shrugged. "I'm sorry, but I don't expect compensation or a contract. I did this for fun and out of concern for my daughter. If the modifications I did can be useful to others, then I'm glad."

"Well, thank you, sir, but we don't work that way. Our idea may have no merit, and Piker no interest—alternatively, if Piker likes the concept, we might sell a couple of thousand units per year. You deserve to take part if that happens. To start, we suggest our shop sponsors the rest of Carrie's trip. The promotion to support the new brand would justify the small investment."

"You're kidding!" exclaimed Carrie. "What would I have to do for that?"

"Nothing more than what you're already doing. We'd slap a logo on your bike and make press announcements about your journey, including pictures of the prototypical Brinkley model in the places you go. We would replace your generic jerseys with new Piker ones, and provide a credit card to pay for food and accommodations. Your adventure will interest people, especially considering the pandemic."

"What do you think, Dad? It sounds unbelievable!"

"I agree, and I like the idea of publicizing the trip. That might make it a little safer. Thanks, Jeff."

"You're welcome, and we'll discuss more details later. As I mentioned, the bike should be ready the day after tomorrow, once we've double-checked that all the electronics still work."

"OK, I won't plan to restart the trip until Friday."

"Good. We might convince the mayor to stage a send-off announcing the bike shop's participation, if you wouldn't mind holding off until ten that morning. The event would surely attract local media, and possibly some regional news outlets."

***

The circumstances responsible for creating and allowing their relationship precluded many customary dating rituals for Carrie and Russ. They biked twice on the Flint Hills Trail in broad daylight, and both of their dinners together were as a group of four with Carrie's parents.

Russ enjoyed Hal and Maddie's company, and never pressured for more intimate outings with Carrie.

If their environment left some desires unfulfilled, neither of them seemed willing to risk failure by moving too fast. Just as good wine should be savored, not gulped, their budding romance could not be fully explored in a few days. Still, the expiring clock on their current time together caused no noticeable anxiety. Both felt they had started something important enough that it needed finishing... just not right now.

When Russ delivered Carrie's repaired bicycle on Thursday evening, she met him in the parking lot. She and her parents would enjoy their last meal together, before she resumed her journey to California, at Russ's home. He had admitted to being an accomplished grille chef the evening before, and promised a Midwest feast of grilled, prime-beef filets and the season's first sweet corn for the occasion.

"The bicycle looks like new," said Carrie. "Thank you! Did you bring the invoice?"

"Sure. Would you like me to roll this to your room?"

"That would be great. I went to the ATM today, so I can pay you back by check or cash."

"Either is fine, but let's discuss that upstairs. I want to explain one of the items on the bill."

After he rolled the bicycle into her room, Russ retrieved a paper slip from his front shirt pocket. "I already settled this invoice with Jeff Carroll this afternoon, and hoped you might allow me to make it a going-away gift."

"Not a chance. How much?"

He presented the invoice with a sheepish smile. "I was afraid you might say that."

The total on the bill amounted to four hundred twenty-five dollars, but a significant item on the list of repairs had been deducted from the final charges. The shop credited a new handlebar costing two-hundred-forty dollars, appearing on a line of the expense summary back on the next line.

"What's this about?" asked Carrie. "Why was the new handlebar removed from the final bill?"

"I covered that charge earlier, Carrie, which is non-negotiable."

"Why not?"

"Because after I dropped your bike at the shop, while you were in the hospital, Jeff thought he could have the bike repaired in a day. He was certain he could straighten the fork and the handlebars at his facility."

"So, why order another handlebar?"

"I insisted on it, and told Jeff I'd pay for the new one. I knew that would hold up the total repair by at least two days."

Carrie burst out laughing. "So, I'm only worth about two hundred dollars for the additional days? I hope you got your money's worth!"

"Not yet, but I'm about to."

The kiss surprised Carrie, but she warmed to it in a single heartbeat, and responded enthusiastically by the second one.

At its conclusion, flushed and breathless, she asked, "What would four hundred dollars have bought you?"

"Can I still negotiate?"

"No. I might never make it to California."

"Kansas is far enough for me."

She smiled and placed her hands on his neck. "Thank you, but you know I'm committed to completing the trip. However, I also plan to eventually finish what we started here."

CHAPTER 21

Jeff Carroll had successfully organized a pandemic-conscious ceremony in less than thirty-six hours. A dais on the courthouse steps outside the City Municipal Building sat between a group of chairs spaced six feet apart. City employees placed traffic cones connected by ribbons in front of the podium, marking safe distances between the masked and standing attendees. A television newscasting crew stood near their equipment truck on the sidewalk, and Mayor Jim Hawley began the press event at ten o'clock, welcoming the crowd and introducing Jeff.

As Jeff announced his company's intention to create a new brand of safety-enhanced touring bicycle, Carrie, sitting to one side of the dais, felt self-conscious. His description of her quest exaggerated its importance in her opinion, especially when most were dealing with the more fundamental issues of a significant health crisis.

Fighting the urge to scream, *Jeff, it's just a bike ride!*, she noticed the audience applauding and focused on her. *Oh no, they expect me to speak!*

Her fear of public speaking equaled her fear of snakes, and now public speaking had moved ahead of snakes, but with no choice, she stood and approached the microphone. As she gazed over the crowd, she took a deep breath.

Aware of Carrie's phobia, her mom placed both hands to her mouth. Her dad braced his wife with an arm and gave his daughter an encouraging wink. Russ stood next to them, smiling beneath his mask and trying to transmit confidence.

"Thank you, Jeff," began Carrie. "And thank you, Mayor and citizens of Ottawa. Three weeks ago, when I planned my cross-country bicycle journey, I had never heard of Ottawa—didn't know the town existed. Today, for a variety of reasons, your community ranks as one of my favorite places in the world."

The audience's spontaneous applause surprised her—and boosted her courage.

"I experienced an unfortunate accident approaching Ottawa, and spent an evening in the Ransom Health Hospital. I received a world-class level of medical attention there, and, as I waited several days for repairs to my bicycle, I met some of the kindest and friendliest people I have ever encountered in my life."

More applause.

"Mr. Carroll's business, Ottawa Bike & Trail, performed the repairs and flattered me with interest in my father's modifications to the bike for my journey. I'm honored to help his brother and him create a new brand of Piker touring bicycle. I'll wear my Piker jersey, and display the logo identifying Mr. Carroll's company and your community, with pride for the rest of my trip."

She stopped as the crowd clapped again.

"The people of this town, our country, and our world travel together today on a more challenging journey than mine, as we feel our way through a devastating medical crisis. Your community helped me continue my bicycle mission, and I believe we'll help each other through the pandemic. I *will* make it to California, and we *will* survive the pandemic together! Thank you."

***

Maddie's eyes misted, and Hal exclaimed to Russ, "Who knew she could do that? Public speaking terrorizes her."

"Couldn't prove it by me," said Russ. "She handled the speech well without even referring to notes. I think your daughter's trip has more to do with what she finds out about herself than what she sees on the road. Maybe things like the speech are part of that."

Hal pondered Russ's observation, glad the young veterinarian had become his daughter's friend. "That could be, but the whole thing scares the bejeezus out of Maddie and me."

"Me too, Hal, but she's on a mission."

***

As her parents and Russ approached, Carrie finished an interview with a TV reporter. After bumping the reporter's fist, she turned to her parents. "Bet that surprised you. How many times have you seen me give a speech?"

Her dad answered, "I'm stunned you did it, but not the least surprised you're skilled at it. When did you find time to prepare a speech?"

"I didn't, Dad! Nobody told me I would speak at this event. If they had, I'd have found a reason to restart my trip earlier. When I realized I couldn't avoid it, it was like being pushed off the diving board. Once you're in the air, you can't fly back. You just have to get ready for the water's impact."

Russ laughed. "Well, you did some quick thinking, then. You hit all the right points, and the crowd adored you."

"They encouraged me from the beginning, and I sensed their energy. You live in a special community here, Russ."

"Yes, I do. I'm glad you noticed."

As Carrie prepared to push off, she embraced first her dad, then her mom, and finally Russ, where she might have lingered a few extra seconds.

***

Norm Sloan watched from inside his rental car. The publicity relating to the rest of Carrie's trip resolved the problem of how to track her, but he suspected the increased attention would make his plan more difficult to achieve.

***

Pedaling west again, Carrie waved at people who lined the streets, feeling energized, exhilarated, and carefree. She hoped her biggest challenges on the journey were now behind her. After surviving an angry dog, dangerous thugs, a severe accident, and public speaking, she wondered what else the trip could possibly throw at her that she couldn't handle.

driving ahead of Brinkley tomorrow to scout for more remote locations along her route in Colorado."

"Fine, but my patience isn't unlimited. Finish this so both of us can get on with our lives."

"If you have a better idea, come back and take care of Brinkley yourself. Your brother made a mess of his attempt, and I can't afford a second one."

"You're right about that, Norm. You can't." The line went dead.

Gritting his teeth and wincing, Sloan picked up the map of Colorado he had been studying when Silky called. He concluded that Carrie's expected travel itinerary through the lonelier mountain roads in Southern Colorado would provide safer geography for what he planned.

The daily updates on the Ottawa Bike & Trail website made monitoring Carrie's journey easy, so in Garden City, Kansas, he planned to leave Carrie behind to survey the route ahead of her. The trip from this part of the state to the foothills of the Rockies would take her five days to complete on a bike, but Sloan could accomplish it in a single day.

He opted to follow her one more day.

CHAPTER 23

Carrie didn't mind the monotony of flat country roads, lined by acres of corn, typical in Kansas. These routes carried light traffic, but after Special Agent Hill's ominous warnings in Ottawa, she studied vehicles coming from behind more intensely now, often capturing photos directly through the handlebar system. She hoped the hit-and-run incident in Ottawa hadn't been intentional, but the remote possibility it was generated an elevated level of awareness.

She called Jeff, and usually Russ, at the end of each riding day. Jeff routinely updated Carrie's progress on the Ottawa Bike & Trail website, and he welcomed the originality of the pictures she provided. A recent photo from Dodge City showed Carrie and her Piker standing at the swinging doors of the Boot Hill Museum. The bicycle and Carrie sported brimmed cowboy hats, and Carrie wore a set of authentic six guns, borrowed from the museum, around her waist.

After the photo appeared on the shop's web page, the Ottawa Herald had called Jeff to request permission to run it in the newspaper with a short story.

"As of this morning, we have something like six hundred likes and over two hundred new subscribers to our page," gushed Jeff. "We're also out of bikes to rent this weekend, and sold six Pikers today."

"Wow! And you think the pictures I posted caused that?"

"I do. People holed-up because of COVID now look for safe things they can do outside. We're just south of a major metropolis, and many folks didn't know a nationally recognized bike trail existed close to them. Almost everybody can ride a bicycle, and your photos, along with the promotion of the cross-country journey, remind them of something available near home."

"I'm delighted, Jeff. Has Piker responded to your proposal yet?"

"Yes. The midwestern sales rep called on Wednesday to tell me the regional vice president requested a reference on our business. She said their board reviewed our submission and had an interest. My brother and

"Hey, Dave," said McCleary. "The twister went right through the house. Never touched the barn, but we could hear what was happening outside from the cellar."

"But the family's all right? Nobody hurt?" asked Dave.

"We're fine. What about you all?"

"We were lucky. The tornado took out an old chicken house we didn't use, and left debris, but damaged nothing else. Why don't you and the family come back to my house? You can call the insurance company from there and stay with us as long as necessary."

McCleary turned his head from the destroyed home to Harrison, staring a few moments before answering. "Thank you, Dave... sincerely. It shouldn't surprise me that you're the first one here to help, and I appreciate that. My brother's on his way over, and we'll stay with him. The family will be OK, but the storm made me think about things. We're fortunate to have only lost the house. Do you know anything about Tribune? How are things in town?"

"Not sure, Caleb. Carrie and I will head over and check. This is Carrie Brinkley, by the way. We found her bicycling to Tribune, and Sallie Jo and I suggested she divert to our storm cellar."

"I think she made the right decision. Thanks for stopping over. It means a lot."

"No problem. You know my cell number if you need me."

During the exchange between Dave and McCleary, Carrie had said nothing, and remained quiet until Dave's pickup cleared McCleary's driveway. "You two must have history."

"A little. We don't agree on politics or religion. Sometimes storms like this one remind you what's important, though."

His nonchalant wisdom landed in Carrie's mind explosively, and she quietly allowed it to brew without responding. The drive to Tribune took fifteen minutes, and damage along the way from the tornado appeared spotty.

The twister touched down toward the middle of one field and cleared a twenty-foot-wide swath as clean as if the corn had been machine harvested. Rows just to the north stood as straight as if they hadn't felt a breeze. Inexplicably, the tornado relocated a large cattle-watering trough to the side of the road, in one piece and undamaged.

"Look at that mess," said Dave as they entered the town limits. Boards and aluminum siding littered one side of a lane; on the other side, four houses sat with no noticeable damage other than debris in the front yards. "Hope those folks made it to the school. That's the emergency cyclone shelter for people without storm cellars."

"Are you telling me houses once sat across the street from those?"

"Yep, four of 'em, exactly like the ones still standing."

"But the siding and lumber on the ground aren't enough for four dwellings. Where's the rest of the material?"

"Scattered over two counties by now. Tornadoes create updrafts strong enough to suck relatively light objects tens of thousands of feet into the air inside the funnel. Let's head to the school and find out what's happening."

Police vehicles, a fire engine, and an ambulance parked in front of an old school boasting 1931 on the upper facing. Many passenger cars and pickup trucks surrounded the emergency vehicles.

Dave pulled into a space and approached a sheriff's deputy stationed at the school's entrance. "Hey, Jason, what's the status here?"

"Hi, Dave. Can't give you much of a report yet. We're still getting calls from out in the county. The storm destroyed the Jiffy Mart west of town and a row of houses on this side. We're receiving multiple reports of damage, but so far, no serious injuries or deaths."

"Hopeful news, I guess. We went past the flattened part of the development on East Lane. Did those folks make it to the shelter?"

"Fortunately, yes. We're making temporary accommodations here at the school for the families who lost their homes. How did the rural areas fare?"

"I didn't see too much," said Dave. "After I checked on the McClearys, I drove straight here. Caleb and Ellen lost their house and will stay with Caleb's brother. The tornado took a chicken house from my property without even leaving debris to clean up. Doesn't seem fair."

"Yeah, well, no intelligent person ever gave Mother Nature credit for having a heart."

"Right. Listen, Jason, can I help with anything? This is my friend Carrie Brinkley, whose bicycle trip to California got interrupted by the tornado."

"Nice to meet you, ma'am. Sorry to welcome you to our community when it looks like this. Dave, if you'd like to check inside with Carolyn, she might have something for you to do."

"I will. Thanks, Jason, and good luck today."

As the two entered the school, Dave told Carrie about the legendary Carolyn Garman. "She's been the high school principal for twenty years, and for twenty years before that, she taught civics. I'm not sure the mayor has more influence around here, and anybody who went to Tribune High School still walks a careful path to avoid her wrong side."

When they returned to the car, Strong said from the driver's seat, "Sorry, Doug. Burns got a little ahead of himself and should have known better."

"But since he didn't, can you enlighten me? What's going on?"

Strong started the car and began driving as he thought. Finally, he spoke. "Look, I had clearance to discuss this with you last week, but wanted to get one final confirmation from Burns this evening. I worried about your disappointment if things didn't work out, and figured you didn't deserve that."

"So, Burns is really FBI?"

"No, not even close. I told you before, as far as I know, he's a Lutheran minister. He's the associate pastor for the church in Compton, but he's also a respected authority on international human trafficking. About five years ago, he helped us to cripple the domestic operations of a dangerous criminal group participating in the trade, and we sponsored a top-secret clearance for him. Since then, he's supported us as a highly regarded confidential resource."

"What does any of this have to do with me?"

"Burns is assisting us in establishing a new group within the agency to target trafficking in our country. We'll collaborate with at least six other national and international enforcement agencies, using tactics and strategies we've never tried before. You heard about some of those during the Greenbrier meetings. The mission of the group, and even its existence, is secret. If you accept the assignment, you're the last member selected for the initial team."

Hill accepted the news with thoughtful silence, and Strong didn't disturb it.

Five miles down the road, he said, "Thank you, Jim. You did this."

"Wrong, Doug. You did. A blip in your career temporarily sidelined you, but you broke records with your performance before that. After impressing the folks sent to assess you at the Greenbrier, you only needed a final check mark from Burns."

"When would the assignment start, and where would the Bureau base me?"

"Anytime in the next ninety days that suits you, and I believe you'll operate out of Reno, Nevada, but that could change. Does it matter to you?"

Yes! Yes! It matters. All of a sudden, it matters! But he responded verbally to his boss, "Of course not."

He arrived back at his apartment in Clarksburg too late in the evening to call Henrietta. While he couldn't share details about the upcoming assignment, Hill had to alert her about the imminent move. The prospects for the new job excited him, but he worried about how it might affect his relationship with Henri, and he resolved to talk to her first thing in the morning.

CHAPTER 26

Carrie started early and, after the most grueling ride of her entire trip yet, reached Westcliffe before noon. The views on the way were dazzling, but she almost cheered when Route 78 connected to the more significant Route 96 two and a half hours into her morning ride.

Coasting into the town from the mountain's elevation to the east buoyed her, and she rallied her strength while eating at a table outside the Bootlegger Deli on Main Street. At 1:00, she felt ready to resume, knowing she had little time to spare to beat the early sundown in the mountains. She was halfway to Salida, confident now she could make the day's scheduled destination.

Route 96 intersected with the smaller Route 1A to connect to Cotopaxi, and Carrie stopped her bike for a brief rest where an even tinier road diverted to the left of Route 1A. Route 35 appeared to be a shortcut, eliminating several miles of biking toward Salida. With her legs beginning to feel like jelly, any mile saved now counted as a blessing. The safety seminar she attended in Charlottesville had warned about the dangers of pushing the body beyond its capabilities.

She decided on Route 35 as a time-saving, muscle-saving, lung-saving solution to her concerns.

Two miles into the detour, concentrating more on tired limbs than the road, Carrie failed to notice loose rocks on her path ahead. She couldn't brake in time to avoid the scattered stones during an effortless and speedy downhill glide. She managed to maneuver between the bigger ones but rolled over an angled rock that catapulted into the chain, and the jolt jarred her. She kept the bicycle upright while coming to a stop, but her heart sank when she examined the damage.

The broken chain now dragged on the road beneath the bike.

She pushed the bike to the side of the road and checked her pannier for the chain tool in the repair kit. She found it immediately, but she'd never used the device. In the Charlottesville safety class, students watched the instructor demonstrate the tool's utility, but no students had taken part in a chain-repair exercise.

No problem. I can handle this.

Most emergency repairs required eliminating a damaged link to reconnect the chain. The repair shortened the chain but allowed a rider to use the bike until a more permanent mend. After working for fifteen minutes, Carrie realized the chain was missing a few links, and she couldn't stretch it far enough to reconnect.

She walked back up the road to the location of the offending rocks. After searching in the dust for an hour for tiny metal pieces, she gave up.

Carrie glanced at her watch, willing her rising anxiety to avoid full-blown and paralyzing panic. When she had backed into the mall's light pole as a teenager, she called her dad to rescue her. Her academic advisor at Virginia Tech had intervened on her behalf after she missed the deadline for completing her senior thesis. A benevolent farmer and his daughter had saved Carrie from serious consequences when an approaching tornado nearly caught her in open ground.

Who could she call now? Zero bars of service on her iPhone silently confirmed the answer.

Literally and figuratively, in the middle of nowhere by herself, she had no means of communicating with anybody. As a twenty-seven-year-old mature woman, could this really represent the first time such a situation had occurred?

What a sheltered life I've lived.

A continued life, sheltered or otherwise, now might depend on her own clear thinking, and she took several deep breaths to calm herself. Part of the reason for taking the cross-country trip in the first place was to discover her ability to manage situations such as this on her own. She had food, water, and bear spray. What more did she need? She laughed at her unspoken joke, surprised to perceive the subliminal impish chuckle of another.

You think this is funny, don't you, Howie? Thanks for showing up.

Two hours had passed in her attempt to repair the bike, and a fix seemed unlikely today. That meant her transportation options comprised walking or hitching a ride in a passing vehicle. Since she had seen no cars on Route 35, that alternative appeared a long shot. The walk back to the larger Route 1A was nearly the same distance as the one to Route 50 and the small community of Cotopaxi, so she chose forward.

By five o'clock, she had only walked another two miles on the steep and marginal road. The panic she held off earlier surged dangerously, and she forced herself to think.

The SUV pulled to a stop, and the uniformed person inside asked, "Are you Carrie Brinkley?"

"Yes, sir. My bike broke down yesterday, and I spent the night beneath a formation of rocks. How did you know my name?"

The ranger smiled. "You're the only one reported missing in this part of the mountains. You have friends who worried when you didn't arrive in Salida last night. Sorry we weren't able to start looking for you until this morning. We hoped you just took a different route and might show up someplace north of here. What happened to your bike?"

"Nothing serious, only a broken chain, but I couldn't ride that way."

"Well, unless you're dead-set on walking to Cotopaxi or Salida, why don't you put your bicycle in the back of the truck? I'll give you a lift."

"Thank you, sir, I'd appreciate that, and am so sorry to cause the trouble."

"It's OK, ma'am. I'm glad we found you. Name's Dockery Jones, by the way. People call me Doc. Excuse me while I radio the others and cancel the search."

"No problem, Doc. Did your department have anyone searching for me during the night?"

"No, sorry. Someone notified us late last night that you didn't arrive at an expected destination. However, we couldn't begin a search until first light this morning. Why?"

"I saw a car pass below my campsite a little after two in the morning and almost tried to flag it down."

"Probably a good thing you didn't. Nobody lives up here, and I'm not sure who would drive on this road in the middle of the night. Maybe a hunter, I guess, but nothin's in season now."

"Yeah, glad I didn't."

Doc joined Carrie at the rear of his vehicle when he completed his call and surveyed the bike. He pointed to the chain and asked, "What caused that?"

"I hit some rocks in the road, and one flew into the chain."

"Bad luck, and this isn't a route you'd get much help."

Carrie laughed. "I didn't see a car all day until the one I just told you about."

"What made you choose this road?"

"Dumb mistake, I guess. On my map, Route 35 appeared to cut off some miles from the same trip on Route 1A."

"It may," said Doc, "but this shortcut adds an hour to the trip—in a four-wheel-drive vehicle."

"In my case, it added a whole day... and one terrifying night."

"I understand, ma'am. I enjoy coming up here to hunt, but normally, I'm dressed in more than shorts and a sports jersey. Also, I fill my backpack with camping gear and carry a 30-30 rifle."

Carrie enjoyed the ride to Salida with Doc. When he dropped her off at the Simple Lodge & Hostel, he asked what she planned to do about her bike. "I'll get on my computer and find the nearest bike shop."

"How will you get the bicycle there?"

"I'll take a taxi or an Uber. Do you know if Salida has a bike shop?"

"Yep, they do, but they don't have cabs and Ubers. I can pick up a new chain for you later today and bring it to the lodge. Salida has several good choices for lunch, and I often come up here from where I work in Pueblo."

Shocked by the hospitality, Carrie said, "I didn't even think about a smaller town like this not having public transportation options. Thank you so much, Doc, but I insist on paying you for your help."

"Unnecessary, ma'am. We stay busy in ski season, but things slow down here during the summer. After lunch, I'll remove the chain and return with either a new or repaired one."

Carrie made a flurry of cellular calls to friends and family after she checked in. Then, she called both the Pueblo Sheriff's Department and the Pueblo Park Ranger headquarters to apologize for the emergency she caused. She provided a complete report to the ranger station on the excellent service supplied by Dockery Jones.

After the calls, Carrie's hunger demanded full attention, so she donned a face mask to walk down the street to the Boathouse. The popular restaurant offered outdoor dining from a deck built on the banks of the Arkansas River, and the idyllic setting didn't seem complete without a margarita to accompany lunch. Her mood lobbied for a second cocktail after her meal, but then she studied the map she had brought.

Her scheduled ride the following day measured only thirty-eight miles but predominantly ascended, uphill to legendary Monarch Mountain. The mammoth peak's summit rose to twelve thousand feet in elevation, and the road there would cover all but the last thousand feet of that. She planned to stay near the top of Monarch Mountain the following evening, before making the exciting descent down Monarch Pass. Tomorrow promised to be stimulating but physically taxing, and prudence eventually trumped temptation for how to spend the rest of the day.

her body in waves as riveting as love, enjoyable as music, and breathtaking as the sunset. Carrie let it sweep her into a euphoric haze, and her face relaxed into a smile when the gratifying tension abated.

She remounted her bike and continued her journey up the mountain mentally aroused and physically energized. While she might never explain what had just occurred, she felt a new kinship with the mountain. It seemed as much a part of her as she was of it, and they now understood each other.

She conquered the ride in about four hours but could have completed it in three. She had taken her time on this ride to enjoy the views. With time to spare, she could catch up with Jeff, her parents, and Russ.

The Monarch Lodge, built mainly to service winter skiers, remained popular for sightseers, bikers, and hikers in the summer. As she checked in, the friendly desk clerk invited her to join a guided hike to the mountain's summit, leaving the lobby at one o'clock, but she politely declined.

Instead, she stretched out on the comfortable bed. A two-hour nap before a late lunch on the restaurant's veranda seemed a better option. She glanced at her cell phone, and four service bars surprised her. Coverage in the mountains had been sporadic, and Carrie presumed little interfered with digital reception at this elevation. After checking in with her parents and Russ, she called Jeff Carroll at Ottawa Bike & Trail.

"Hey, Carrie! How was the ride to Monarch?"

"Strenuous, Jeff, but the bike performed like a beast up the mountain, and I got here in under four hours."

"Excellent! Take another picture up there — with the Piker if you can. The photo we posted yesterday is still getting likes, and the Boathouse called us about sponsorship."

"Sure, I'll do that. The folks in Salida were charming, and the restaurant owner told me that hikers and bicyclists kept them going in the summer. I didn't ask why she wanted your information, but she seemed interested in my journey."

"How bad does the pandemic impact retail and restaurant businesses in the area?"

"They feel it," answered Carrie. "But Help Wanted signs appeared in the windows of all the restaurants I passed, and few seats remained on the outdoor deck of the Boathouse when I visited. I also saw several people picking up takeout orders at the entrance."

"How about on the mountain? Does the lodge have much business?"

"Not a lot. The front desk person invited me to join a hike this afternoon, but I didn't think I needed additional exercise. While I ate lunch, I watched two mountain bikers going down one of the ski slopes. Have you ever done that?"

"Yes, and it's a memory! You might want us to put some bigger tires on the Piker before you try it, though."

"Right. Maybe next trip."

"Listen, a friend of ours owns a bike shop in Gunnison, and he wondered if you would stop by for some pictures at his place. Will you have time for that?"

"I think so. It's only forty-four miles to Gunnison, all downhill, so I'll arrive early in the afternoon. How far away from the Days Inn is the shop?"

"Don't worry about that. Steve Downing, the bike shop's owner, will pick you up and take you to his store. He and his wife also insist on treating you to dinner."

"OK. No problem. Text me Downing's contact information, and I'll call him when I arrive."

***

Carrie couldn't sleep past seven the following day, and checked out of the Lodge before eight. She coasted downhill to the main gate, never pumping the pedals, and stopped before entering Monarch Pass for a deep breath.

After a long gaze down the winding road, she said, "Here goes!"

As she rounded a steep bend, she noted and recognized the familiar red Ford Focus in the handlebar camera.

OK. That's it, fella'. Now you're officially scaring me!

Carrie estimated her speed at about twenty-five miles per hour, in a zone with a posted limit of forty-five for cars, but the Focus wouldn't pass her. On a straight stretch of road, she clicked a button on the handlebar camera to take a still photo of the car behind her. For insurance, she snapped three more shots. This morning, no other traffic traveled the road, and the red vehicle maintained a consistent distance in back of her, sometimes closing the gap at the broader curves.

Suddenly, a rage of emotions set off an internal explosion, and Carrie decided to take control of the situation. While swerving into an overlook, she gripped the brakes on the handlebar tightly and stopped abruptly. She grabbed a pepper spray canister and squared herself to the highway and the car that followed her.

In the privacy of his cubicle, Hill smiled. He liked this girl. "How about if we do this? Stay where you are for a day, and I'll try to get a look at those files on your home computer. We'll also try to determine Sloan's location—and go from there. I'd feel more comfortable if you stayed out of sight for a little while. Sloan could still be in your general area, and if he's confident you didn't recognize him, he might try something else."

"I can do that," agreed Carrie. "Let's talk again tomorrow."

"Deal."

CHAPTER 30

Before Hill could punch in the number for the Norfolk office, Jim Strong took the seat across from him. "Got a minute, Doug?"

"Sure, Jim. What's up?"

"I informed the necessary people you would like ninety days to finish things here, then report for your next assignment by December. Does that sound about right?"

"Yeah, the timeline will work for me if it works for you. Are you allowed to tell me who I'll report to?"

Jim laughed. "I can, but I hope it doesn't scare you off from the transfer. You'll work directly for *Bluntforce* on a small team led by *Angel*. Your mission is code-named *Night Landing*."

Hill waited for more, but Jim said nothing. "That's it?"

"Scary, isn't it? And someone way up our food chain warned that our agency classifies everything I just told you top secret. Don't share it with anyone."

"We still work for the FBI, right? The President didn't fold us into the CIA, did he?"

"Don't think so, Doug. Whatever *Night Landing* is, nobody uses real names, locations, or unit designations. Since Tom Burns seems involved, we can guess the operation has to do with a human trafficking initiative, but it's so confidential that few at even our highest levels of command know about it."

"I bet a valid reason exists for the secrecy. No problem. Someone will let me know what I need to know when it's time for me to know."

"Right," agreed Strong. "Sorry I can't tell you more."

"I appreciate what you did to put me in line for the opportunity. Back to the present, though. Would you have a good contact in Norfolk? I need an agent to accompany someone to a witness's condo to check a computer."

"Sure, Carl Sales, the Associate Special Agent in Charge. He and I went to the Academy together. I'll text his number."

When Strong left, Hill sat for a moment, considering the strange conversation. Professional agents learned to live in a world of secrets:

didn't I look for Teresa's email in my Gmail trash bin? No, I didn't empty it, and I'm searching for it on my laptop right now."

After a momentary pause, she said, "Here it is! I found the message — and the attachments! As we speak, I'm placing the folder back on my laptop's desktop."

"Could you also forward it to me?" asked Hill.

"Yes, I'm sending it now. Tell me when you get it."

Within a minute, Hill announced, "Got it! Do you notice anything unusual in the folder's documents?"

"Not that much, but I just opened them," admitted Carrie. "One spreadsheet lists the balances of all Pilgrim Burgers' various bank accounts back in June, which shows extra cash because of the COVID loans. The other two files relate to the backup data for Sloan's request for the government-backed loans."

"Right. The two documents don't contain the same numbers."

"One looks like Teresa's spreadsheet, listing several months of payroll data and an estimate of future payroll needs. The other appears to be the government document completed for the loans."

"The payroll documentation on the Excel spreadsheet doesn't match the same information on the loan request," said Hill.

"No, not even close. Teresa provided lower estimates than those submitted, which she likely wanted to show me. Sloan didn't use the data she created."

"We're missing something. I need to think about this. It's illegal to get a loan using falsified information, but I can't understand why your knowledge of that would justify a solution as extreme as murder. Why would Brown or Sloan chase you all over the country for this? For the moment, it doesn't matter. This warrants picking Sloan up for questioning, which will make your life safer."

"OK," said Carrie, not sounding so sure. "I'm sorry for making the problem more complicated than needed."

"Can you stay put for another day or so? I don't believe it will take long to find Sloan."

"Sure. Thank you."

After the conversation with Hill, Carrie mentally searched for a sense of relief — and came up empty. Evil people had followed her from Virginia, intent on ending her life. Now, thanks to Special Agent Hill and his team, that might soon stop, so she should feel happy. Why didn't she?

As she surveyed the spreadsheets open on her laptop, she remembered the stress in Teresa Dill's voice when they talked on the phone. Then she recalled her anguish about Teresa's disappearance, and Sloan's cockiness on his call to her in Grundy.

Like an awful slide show, the vision of a Jeep running her off the road near Ottawa transitioned to one of a red car stalking her in Kansas to the image of trees on a winding mountain highway in Colorado. An uncomfortable sensation in her stomach blossomed past her heart to her head.

Unlike the customary self-conscious whispers from her soul that usually guided her, this emotion roared — bold, powerful, and unafraid. An inner voice thundered in anger: *Fight!* Carrie's fingers responded to a mental command she didn't remember giving — tapping out the numbers for Hill's cell phone.

"Special Agent Hill speaking."

"Hi, Agent Hill. This is Carrie again, and I've done some thinking about our conversation. Do you have a minute?"

"Sure, Carrie. What's up?"

"If you arrest Sloan on suspicion of falsifying information about a loan document, even if convicted, he'll earn a mild penalty. Right?"

"Depending on several factors, yes. The disclosure violation is a relatively minor offense, and he might pay a fine but not face jail time."

"Well, that makes me angry! We're pretty sure he has something to do with Teresa Dill being missing, and we think he had plans to kill me yesterday. I don't want to spank him — I want to hang him!"

"Understood, Carrie, but getting him off the street protects you. We may also convince him to talk about his involvement in more serious crimes by arresting him on the minor charge."

"Or, by alerting him he's under scrutiny, he could double down on his efforts to conceal other crimes. You told me you have zero physical evidence connecting him to Teresa Dill's disappearance."

"True, but I'm developing a theory about what happened and why. I need a little more information to solve the Dill case, though."

"So, why don't we buy you some time for additional research? Sloan isn't aware we identified him yesterday, but he'll become suspicious if my trip stops suddenly. He's currently plotting a crime terrible enough to net him years in prison, if you catch him in the act, but you may not catch him at anything more serious than a minor disclosure violation by picking him up for questioning."

"True, but the FBI doesn't use innocent citizens as bait. I'm also convinced Sloan had something to do with Teresa Dill's disappearance. And, let's face it, she isn't only missing. She's almost surely dead. We just

As Carrie waited on a sofa beneath an artificial tree limb holding a cougar ready to pounce, she wondered at the connection between taxidermy and cell phone repair in Montrose. Her instincts told her she was missing something here, and she made a mental note to query Agent Hill.

The shop's owner returned to Carrie fifteen minutes later with two cell phones in her hand. "All data from old phone now in new one," she said, "and small device attached under front fender of bike outside. You be safer now because people know where are."

"Wow, that was quick. Thank you. Besides the taxidermy, do you provide cell phone and electronics services for the community here?"

"No," answered the woman succinctly.

Caught off-guard by the short answer, Carrie said, "I see. Well, I love your shop. Does someone local create these magnificent displays?"

"No. Only me."

"My goodness! These are museum quality! Did you go to school to learn how to do this?"

"No. Just always good with knives."

While this unique woman possessed unusual skills, she was not a conversationalist. If she had an interesting history, Carrie would not learn it today. "How much do I owe you for your work, ma'am?"

"Nothing. Somebody else pay. Be careful."

Carrie thanked the woman and left, full of questions for Special Agent Hill. Someone had provided the Asian woman with information about Carrie, but Carrie knew no more about her than the moment she'd entered the shop.

***

Norm Sloan rested in Provo, Utah, over three-hundred-fifty miles away. His misfire on Monarch Pass had convinced him he needed a different approach, and his new strategy involved a high-powered rifle equipped with a scope. Selecting a suitably remote location also appeared simple. Places meeting that requirement littered the part of the country Carrie Brinkley would bike through west of Provo. Disappointed his mission was taking longer than expected, Sloan remained galvanized by Silky's threat to expose him.

He called his Vice President of Operations to explain the delay. "Yeah, sorry, Oscar. I hadn't planned such an extended trip, but a friend offered me this once-in-a-lifetime opportunity to elk hunt in Utah with him. Your excellent reports show me nothing critical I need to handle back there."

"Well," said Fittipaldi, "no emergencies, but we have a few issues. The Hampton and Suffolk units can't cover payroll this week, and two other stores will be tight. Dawn thinks balances from COVID loans exist someplace, but I can't find these in accounts at headquarters."

"No, I moved those funds over to investment accounts to hold until we needed them. Sorry, I forgot about leaving instructions for accessing the money. Do this: tell Dawn to cancel the direct deposit for my salary this month, and use the extra funds to remedy shortfalls until I return. I shouldn't be more than another ten days or so."

"OK. That will cover it for now. I might borrow from one or two of the units with positive balances to offset the deficits in others. Dawn says you don't like complicating our books, though."

"I don't, but in an emergency, it's OK. I'll straighten everything out when I'm back. We carry overdraft coverage with our banks, so any shortfalls convert to short-term loans. We should try to avoid running up interest charges if we can."

"So, you think you'll return here a week after next?" asked Fittipaldi.

"Something like that. It depends on a couple of things, but I'll keep you posted. Did you hire one of the CFO candidates?"

"No. Do you want me to pick one without you interviewing?"

"Well, I don't think you should let a qualified contender get away from us while you wait for me. How about we set up a Zoom interview with your top three choices tomorrow?"

"We can do that. What time should I set up the meetings?"

"Schedule any time after 2:00 PM eastern time, and I'll dial in."

Sloan sensed Fittipaldi's irritation and regretted the circumstances responsible for the young man's frustrations. Fittipaldi now supervised a twenty-one-unit franchise without the benefit of a CEO, CFO, or IT manager, during one of the most challenging times in the country's history for hospitality industries. Unfortunately, Sloan couldn't presently help much as he concentrated on the greater priority of avoiding jail. If he could manage that, he'd repair any short-term damages to his company later.

Utah required no permit to buy a rifle, only a criminal background check, and finding a weapon for Sloan's purposes proved easy. Mountain Gun & Ammo, however, didn't stock the high-powered, deluxe scope Sloan preferred for the selected rifle. To avoid losing the sale, the owner assured Sloan another store would deliver the desired scope by the

CHAPTER 33

Carrie picked up immediately when her cell phone rang. "Hi, Agent Hill. Where are you?"

"Maybe fifteen minutes from Green River. Can we still meet this evening?"

"Yes. When and where?"

"How about the Super 8, and we'll eat at the Tamarisk Restaurant a block from the motel. I'm staying there tonight as well."

"Sounds fine, but you're aware I'm limited to biking clothes for wardrobe, right? Is the Tamarisk fancy?"

"No, and with the COVID restrictions on spacing, they don't take many reservations. I took a chance and requested an outside table for 6:30. Can you make that?"

"Certainly. I only have to change into fresh shorts and a T-shirt. Knock on the door when you're ready. I'm in #112."

***

When Carrie answered the door, the man on the other side apologized as he flashed his creds. "Sorry, Carrie, the blue sports coat may seem dressy, but it's sort of the standard attire for our group. I didn't change from my meeting in Provo this afternoon."

The agent was younger than Carrie expected.

"I understand, Agent Hill, and as long as you don't mind going into the restaurant with a chick in biker shorts and a T-shirt, I'm fine. I doubt anyone looking will mistake which one of us is the FBI agent."

"That obvious?"

"Right out of a B-level movie."

"Oh well." Hill laughed. "I'm armed if we meet any smart alecks."

"Great. I won't bring my pepper spray, then. Shall we go?"

At the restaurant, Carrie ordered a beer before the meal, and Hill, who insisted Carrie call him Doug, requested tea.

"Crap! Sorry, Doug. You can't drink on duty, can you? I didn't think about that when I ordered the beer."

"No problem at all. I *am* on duty, but you enjoy the beer. I don't drink... anymore."

Hill came from Kentucky, and the two laughed about Carrie cycling past his hometown and college. He told her about the communities sharing her first and last name near his town, and the coincidence amused her.

"I can't believe I didn't notice towns with those names so close to my route when I researched the trip."

"They're so small they may not show up on your maps," answered Hill. "What did you think of Berea?"

"I loved it, and want to return when I can spend more time. What a fascinating history for the college!"

"It's a unique place," admitted Hill. "I got lucky when somebody recommended me for acceptance."

Carrie sensed Hill's youth might have been intriguing, but he changed the subject.

"Norman Sloan purchased a high-powered rifle, which is why I visited Provo today."

Carrie covered her mouth in surprise. "Did you arrest him?"

"No. No laws prevent purchasing a weapon like that in Utah, but it requires a criminal background check. The gun shop's request for the search triggered a report, and I came to Utah to witness Sloan pick up the rifle."

"Something tells me you have more to your story," said Carrie.

"Yes. He arrived in the same red Ford Focus he had on the Monarch Pass, and I monitored him from the parking lot as he went inside. While he completed his transaction in the store, I placed a small GPS tracking device under his front bumper. Look at this." Hill retrieved his cell phone.

On the screen of Hill's phone, a map showed two illuminated dots. Hill expanded the map with his fingers, and Carrie could read street names. "So that dot marks the location of Sloan's car?"

"Yes. He's still in Provo, but I can track him wherever he goes. He purchased the gun legally, and we have no reason to pick him up. People buy those kinds of guns to hunt elk, but I suspect he doesn't plan to use the rifle for sport."

"So, what now? I noticed another lighted dot on the screen before you expanded the map. Is that your car?"

***

"Hi, Doug. I made it."

"I was beginning to worry because it's after six. Rough trip?"

"Yes, very. I underestimated the route and overestimated my ability. Dangerous combination."

"I'm sorry. You OK?"

"Yes. Ecstatic. The Super 8 here has a tub, not just a shower, and I'm enjoying a hot bath with a Corona Light I bought at the 7-11 next door."

"Wonderful! What's for dinner tonight?"

"I told you, Doug. A Corona light, icy, with another one waiting for dessert. I'm too exhausted to eat, and the beer tastes really good tonight, particularly with protein bars and almonds. I'll sleep in tomorrow, and plan to order a big takeout breakfast from the diner down the street. The ride from here to Delta should take under five hours, so tomorrow won't be so bad."

"Good for you. Your old friend is settling into Fallon, and I'm not far away in a different motel. He spent a lot of time today on Route 50 between Austin and here, so I think he's narrowing down his location for a sniper attempt."

"If I stay on my schedule, I'm about four days away from Austin, right?" asked Carrie.

"Yeah, maybe five, depending on whether you make it to Baker in one day from Delta. Don't press yourself. The Ottawa website posts your daily progress, and I'm sure that's what Sloan monitors to track your location. You can choose a comfortable pace."

"I understand, but unfortunately, the availability of overnight accommodations along this part of the route determines my pace. None exist between Delta and Baker, and I've found I'm not a camping enthusiast. I'll rest well in Delta tomorrow and try to make it to the Border Inn in Baker."

"OK, and you also have a backup now. I can always retrieve you wherever you are."

"I guess, but I don't want to raise Sloan's suspicions now. We're too close to catching him. Have you figured out why he thinks the files Teresa sent me are so important?"

"Not completely, but I have a theory," said Hill, "as well as added information to support it."

"You planning to keep it a secret?"

"No. Finding Damien Brown's car abandoned in Kansas City gave us a name with an extensive history in several of our databases. We do our best to maintain accurate records on former felons—like current addresses, employment, and other civil infractions. After we found the reservation he made to return to Norfolk from Kansas City, his name appeared on a Southwest manifest for a flight from Norfolk to Cuba through Miami. His sister took the same flight."

"They went to Cuba? Is that legal?"

"Not for Damien, not without the government's permission. He's an ex-felon, but that wouldn't prevent him from obtaining a legal passport. There would be no problem for his sister. Travel to Cuba only requires a passport and a Cuban Tourist Card, and flights regularly leave from the United States. Visitors can stay for up to four weeks on the card."

"What happens after that?"

"They're supposed to come home, but Cuba's enforcement can be lax. People with money can sometimes convince officials to extend their stay."

"What does this have to do with Sloan?"

"Sloan and Brown most likely conspired to steal the COVID money your former company received, and Dill may have threatened to expose the fraud. When they discovered Dill took files with her after being fired, they killed her. Sylvia's brother likely did the dirty work. After that, Sylvia decided she no longer needed Sloan and took the money and her brother to Cuba."

"So why wouldn't Sloan call you guys and tell them about Brown?" asked Carrie.

"Because Brown would implicate him in his participation in, or knowledge of, the murder of Dill. Remember, she's in Cuba, where she believes we can't touch her. Sloan isn't. If Sloan can clean up the loose end relating to you, Brown might feel confident authorities might never discover the COVID loan fraud. Sloan will someday pay off that loan from normal corporate profits and avoid jail as an accessory to murder. Sylvia and her brother could safely return to the United States after that. I think Brown is blackmailing Sloan."

"Clever."

"Exactly," said Hill. "Sloan must be livid Brown stole nine million dollars from him, but no statute of limitation exists for murder, and he wants to avoid jail at any cost."

"Wow. Complicated."

"Yep, but Brown confounded the strategy to her disadvantage. We were at a dead end on Dill, and nobody in the government had reason to

"No shit, Einstein! Exactly like I signed most of the company's disbursements for the past year. Did you forget you were too lazy to bother with the checks every Friday afternoon and required me to handle those? I doubt any handwriting expert who compares the signatures on your company's checks to this one will see a difference—because there isn't one. Three of us carried corporate credit cards, and I bet if someone searched Dill's condo, they'd find hers. Did you remember to take it back?"

"No, and so what? Why did you call? You can't blackmail me more than you already have. For your information, I'm near Reno, still trailing Brinkley, and don't need your bullshit threats to keep distracting me!"

"I wouldn't label my calls threats, Norman, just friendly warnings. I also thought it important for you to see an example of what I can provide if it ever becomes necessary. By the way, you should delete the message I sent and the JPEG, because you wouldn't want somebody to discover it on your phone. Complete this last little detail with Brinkley, and we can forget all about my evidence and additional calls. You'll never hear from me again."

"I'm working on it, and I'll finish this week," muttered Sloan.

"What the hell is taking so long? You've been at it for a month."

"And your professional criminal brother, with more experience at these things than me, took almost three weeks—and failed. A fatal hit-and-run isn't easy to execute, and it took me less time to figure that out than Damien. I decided on a different and more reliable plan."

"OK, so what is it?"

"Not one I'm willing to share. You can learn what you need to know by monitoring the newspaper."

"Fair enough, Norman, but my patience is wearing thin."

"So is mine."

Sloan angrily threw his cell phone to the bed—then remembered the JPEG he'd downloaded. He deleted the file, emptied the iPhone's trash bin, and cleaned the cache. Everything Silky had told him, unfortunately, was accurate. *Of course*, the credit card receipt signature would match thousands of signatures on as many checks he had supposedly signed.

How could he have been so stupid—and so wholly underestimate Silky? He'd wanted nothing to do with Teresa Dill's disappearance, so he asked for none of the details. Silky made sure he had those, though. On an anonymous tip, authorities would drag the Elizabeth River at a designated spot, and no doubt find the body. They would also recover bolt cutters, a handcart, and a logging chain.

Shit!

Carrie Brinkley gave no sign she either understood what the files Dill took from the company contained, nor cared. Sloan couldn't understand Silky's obsession with eliminating her, but she hadn't given him a vote in the decision. He genuinely regretted what happened to Teresa Dill, and hated himself for the crime he now contemplated. Regrettably, his freedom depended on Brinkley's death.

He retrieved the map and surveyed the various marks on it. He circled his top three selected locations using a red pen, and determined to perform a last detailed examination the following day.

CHAPTER 36

Sloan's answers didn't satisfy Silky, especially considering her failure to find a crooked immigration official. Despite bribe offers that escalated daily, she had identified no agent willing to extend her travel card again. With only a short time until the current period expired, she needed to make some crucial decisions.

Only Sloan could indisputably connect her to Teresa Dill's disappearance. If Carrie Brinkley had any suspicions, her evidence was entirely circumstantial or based on hearsay. Eliminating the former IT manager might be convenient, but probably not critical. Sloan, however, could be a significant problem if Silky and Damien had to return to the states. His evidence would be highly damaging if he ever lost the incentive to hide it.

Sloan would face a jail sentence if the government discovered his COVID money fraud, and Silky was certain he would divulge her role in the scheme if that happened. When Brinkley seemed to be the last one who might precipitate an investigation into the financial crime, Silky forced Sloan into a plan to prevent that possibility. Now, she wished she hadn't, because Sloan would also lose the inducement to protect Silky if authorities arrested him for homicide. Since he wasn't an accomplished and competent criminal, the odds of that outcome were better than she cared for.

It now crystalized for her: Brinkley didn't represent the weak link in this chain; Sloan did. Even if he succeeded in his current efforts with Brinkley, he *might* become a liability later. If authorities discovered a murder he committed, or caught him in the attempt, he *would* be a liability.

Silky had hoped living in a country with no extradition agreements with the United States might make such considerations irrelevant, but she now had to contemplate the ramifications of returning to the states. The obvious solution to her problem was to take Sloan entirely out of the equation before he made a stupid mistake in his plans for Brinkley.

With her most practical course now clear, she opened her computer to check flights from Havana.

A day later, Damien confessed confusion about Silky's plan as they waited in the departure area for the Southwest flight to Miami.

"I don't get it, Sis. We have a boarding pass, so why look for another couple with tickets?"

"We aren't getting on this flight, Damien. We'll find people who look a bit like us, then trade passports and travel documents for 500,000 pesos."

"That's over twenty thousand dollars," exclaimed Damien. "Why would we do that?"

"To provide enough incentive for them to make the exchange. Not forever—only until they arrive in Miami. After that, they'll mail ours back to us, and we'll send theirs to them."

"Won't they get in trouble?"

"Customs agents only glance at passport photos and retrieve the disembarkation declaration completed on the airplane. The couple will probably pass through with no problem, and at worst, might have to explain that someone accidentally switched their passport at the check-in counter."

"Won't they suspect we're criminals and hesitate to switch, even for lots of cash?"

"Maybe, but I'll tell them we only want to stay in their wonderful country, and the temporary switch will accomplish that. Once Customs electronically records our passports back in the United States, we satisfy the stipulations of our travel cards. If the wrong people *are* waiting for us when our surrogates go through Customs, they won't find us. For most Cubans, twenty thousand dollars is a lot of money, and the risk of getting caught is small... as long as nobody is specifically watching for us in Miami."

"OK," said Damien. "I guess that might work, but why go to all the trouble and waste twenty thousand dollars?"

"Just exercising caution, which doesn't end with only switching passports. We're taking the new passports to a different gate later this afternoon, where we'll purchase the existing boarding passes of two people planning to take the Havana flight to Houston. I figure a twenty-five-hundred-dollar profit per ticket should suffice for those boarding passes."

"OK. I'm lost. If authorities might wait for us in Miami, why wouldn't they also wait in Houston?" asked Damien.

"Because our names won't appear on any airline manifest for Houston, and we'll clear Customs under the identities of whoever we find to trade passports this morning."

"How will we determine if the couple with our passports gets through in Miami?"

"We don't care. If they clear Customs, or only get stopped because of the mix-up, great. We wasted twenty thousand dollars on insurance. If our reservation for Miami prompts a response from law enforcement, we'll be in Houston."

"Clever. So, we won't be in Miami or Cuba, and no record of us in Houston. Where then?"

"Reno, where Sloan is."

***

The combination of Silky Brown's expiring Cuban Travel Card and the reservation for a flight from Havana to Miami triggered an alert to the CJIS in West Virginia. After Special Agent Hill discovered Brown's absence from her job in Virginia, he entered her name as a "person of interest" relating to the missing persons case of Teresa Dill in the facility's massive database. He'd also included Sylvia's brother, Damien.

His recent request to the FAA Enforcements Division resulted in an alert about Brown's airline reservation for the Havana flight. The report of her scheduled departure passed from CJIS to the laptop Hill carried with him in Nevada.

"Hi, Jim," said Hill, calling from his motel in Fallon. "I just received a notice that Sylvia Brown and her brother are listed on a flight scheduled to leave Havana tomorrow. Could you coordinate some assets on the ground in Miami?"

"Sure, Doug. You're pretty sure they're responsible for Dill, right?"

"We're certain Damien Brown abandoned his jeep at the Kansas City airport after Carrie Brinkley's accident in Ottawa. We also have confirmation that approximately nine million dollars resulting from COVID relief loans, which used to sit in Pilgrim Burgers' banks, is no longer there. Pilgrim Burgers' CEO, Norman Sloan, followed Carrie Brinkley from Kansas and purchased a high-powered rifle in Utah for no reason. I suspect Brown is coercing or somehow blackmailing him into eliminating Brinkley. They're worried Brinkley has information that could connect them to Dill's disappearance."

"But, so far, the evidence we have tying the Browns to either Dill's disappearance or embezzlement is all circumstantial, right?"

"Yes, but we have valid reasons to pick them up for questioning. I doubt the Browns intended on coming back to the states. Their Travel

Cards expire soon, and they probably couldn't buy off an official to fix that. They won't hang around our country long with access to the kind of money they stole, so we may not get too many additional opportunities to talk to them."

"I agree, Doug. Good work. I'll call Miami. What's Sloan up to?"

"He's narrowing down his options for a sniper location. I can track everywhere he travels, and I think we have a solid plan to catch him."

"And we're keeping Brinkley safe?"

"Yes. We communicate almost every evening, and I briefed her on the operational plan. I track her movements daily through the device attached to her bike."

"OK. I'll text you when I receive a confirmation from Miami."

***

The following day, a message from Customs didn't surprise agents stationed within the terminal at Miami International Airport. The bureau had warned Customs and Border Protection officials to flag the passports of Damien and Sylvia Brown after the flight from Havana landed. As two federal agents crossed the chain into the secure Customs area, they saw an agent wave to them from the last booth in the line of checkpoints. A distressed couple stood with the Customs officer outside of the booth.

After flashing official identification, one of the Bureau agents asked the Customs official, "Are these the Browns?"

"No, sir. This is Julio and Amara Martinez. They say the ticketing agent in Havana mixed up their passports."

"Can we find out if someone from this flight presented the Martinez's passports?"

"We already know that nobody has. All other passengers from the flight have cleared."

The federal agent focused on the more upset member of the couple, Mrs. Martinez. "Ma'am, can you explain how a ticketing agent inadvertently handed you the wrong passport?"

Julio answered the question for his distressed wife. "No, sir. I am sorry, but we did something very wrong. A woman paid us over 500,000 pesos to switch passports. She said she wanted to stay in Cuba beyond the dates specified on her Travel Card."

"Thank you, sir, for your honesty. You committed a federal crime, and I must charge you, but I will note your cooperation in my report. Do you believe the people with your passports remained in Cuba?"

"I can't answer that, *señor*. I don't know."

"What is your citizenship?"

"We are Cuban, *señor*."

***

In West Virginia, Special Agent Jim Strong took the call from Miami.

"We have a problem in Miami, sir."

"What's that?" asked Strong.

"The Browns switched passports with another couple in Cuba, and didn't arrive on the flight to Miami."

"Damn! What about the couple with the Browns' passport? Did they show up on any other manifests out of Havana?"

"Their names are Julio and Amara Martinez, and no. Nobody with those names flew from Havana yesterday."

"So," asked Strong, "you think the Browns stayed in Cuba?"

"We don't know, sir, but it seems odd they would bother switching passports if they didn't plan to travel."

"Right. Can we keep checking flights over the next few days for signs of anyone named Martinez on a manifest?"

"We can review all manifests for incoming flights from Cuba, based on suspicion of passport fraud, but we won't receive much help from the Cuban side. If the Browns either went or plan to go to an alternative international destination, we'll need to jump through some different hoops for help."

"I understand. Thank you."

After hanging up, Strong surveyed the map of the United States on his wall. After a moment, he pressed the intercom on his desk telephone. "Trudi, find Lydell and send him up here right away!"

Lydell Trudal, sixty-five, coordinated over twenty-five private and commercial databases for CJIS. He'd retired from the Navy as a security analyst twenty years earlier, and had been a senior manager at the CJIS facility since its inception. Lydell proudly told everyone at CJIS that he didn't plan to retire for another thirty years.

"What's up, Jim?"

"I'm unfamiliar with the rules for accessing airline records, but I need to find out if Julio and Amar Martinez traveled today from any airport in the United States that hosts inbound flights from Cuba."

"That shouldn't be difficult with a legal reason for the information. Not that many cities offer direct flights from Havana."

"Would passport fraud qualify? Two suspected criminals are using the Martinez's passports."

"Sure. A federal crime works. Give me the spelling of the names, and I'll start a query in the International Air Transport Association database. Do you want me only to check flights leaving today?"

"Today, and possibly for the next few."

"Got it. I'll call you if I find something."

Within an hour, Strong received a call from Trudal. "Hey, Lydell. Any luck?"

"Yep, at the third airport we checked, Houston. Mr. and Mrs. Martinez booked a two o'clock direct flight to Reno and, with the time zone change, landed out there at four."

"Excellent, Lydell. I can't thank you enough. Do you have a theory about why the Martinez names didn't show up on the incoming flight to Houston?"

"They either had a third set of passports with different names, or bought somebody's boarding pass for the Houston flight in Havana. The Customs agent in Houston isn't required to compare a boarding pass to a passport. They generally only check the passport and the Customs Declaration Form completed by passengers during the flight. If the Browns appeared remotely like the Martinez couple, the Browns could pass through."

"I hadn't thought about the possibility of purchasing someone else's boarding pass. Thanks again."

Strong glanced at his watch as he called Hill. Intercepting the Browns at the Reno airport would not be possible.

"Hill here."

"Hey, Doug, it's Jim. We had problems in Miami today. The Browns switched passports with another couple and didn't show up in Miami."

"Shit. Any idea where they went?"

"Yes. Reno. They flew from Cuba to Houston without showing up on an airline manifest. Most likely, they purchased someone's boarding passes with cash in Havana, but didn't have time to do the same for the Reno flight. They landed there about a half-hour ago using the identification of the couple they switched passports with in Havana. We couldn't schedule an intercept that quickly."

"That's still useful information. Thanks. I don't like their proximity to Sloan today."

"What do you think they're up to?" asked Jim.

"Hard to say, but the fact they chose Reno isn't a coincidence. Silky could be communicating with Sloan, or perhaps they guessed Carrie's and Sloan's location based on the biking itinerary they stole from Carrie's computer. Their Travel Cards probably expired in Cuba, and they couldn't bribe the right person for a new one."

"You said Sloan was about to implement his plan for Carrie. Do you think the Browns flew in to help?"

"Possibly, but why cut it so close? I think Sloan plans to pull the trigger, metaphorically and literally, tomorrow. Brown's target may be Sloan. Silky won't make a stupid mistake like using a credit card, so locating her brother and her might be difficult."

**

When they landed in Reno, Silky and Damien walked straight from the terminal to a line of Ubers outside. "Take us to the closest used car lot still open," she ordered.

The driver queried his GPS and headed south from the airport, stopping several miles later at Ponderosa Used Cars. Silky paid him cash and told him not to wait.

After surveying the selection of junky-looking automobiles, she asked the sales agent, who also doubled as the owner of the business, about a later model Jeep Liberty with no price sticker glued to the windshield.

"We haven't processed that one to inventory. We just got it yesterday."

The vehicle had California tags and a fresh inspection sticker. "How many miles on it?" asked Silky.

"Only 65,000, but as I told you, I can't sell it yet. The owner couldn't locate the title."

"Right," said Silky, "because he stole the car, and you haven't had time to forge counterfeit documents. Listen, I don't care about that. How much for the vehicle?"

Embarrassed that Silky caught him at his scam, the man answered, "Well, with not a scratch on it and a solid engine, this vehicle will sell for between twelve and fifteen thousand dollars."

"But without a title, it ain't worth shit. Fill the gas tank, and I'll give you seven thousand in cash."

"Let me get the keys."

On the road in their new ride, Damien asked his sister, "What now?"

"A quick stop at Walmart for some clothes and a couple of cheap cell phones, then a comfortable motel for the night. We'll call Sloan tomorrow."

"What if he's already taken care of Brinkley?"

"All the better. If he was successful, he's already returned to Virginia, and we'll head south to San Diego. From there, I'll find a private pilot to take us someplace over the border."

"And if he hasn't finished with her?"

"Then we'll tell him we're here to help."

"But we won't?"

"No. We'll shut him up before he has a chance to get caught in the attempt."

"And then find Brinkley ourselves?"

"Nope. With Sloan out of the way, we won't worry about Brinkley. She might have some evidence about Sloan's financial scam, but we aren't on her radar. If we were safe in Cuba, we wouldn't care whether Sloan got caught because our government couldn't touch us. Now, though, Sloan's the only one who can connect us to Dill. If he's apprehended for attempted murder, he won't hide our role in Dill's disappearance."

"So, if we eliminate him, why go someplace out of the country?"

"Extra precaution. Somebody up here could get lucky and start putting the puzzle together, and if that happens, we would be safer in a foreign country. With a boatload of cash, that won't be difficult. The suitcase contains almost half a million dollars, and we can access an offshore account with a balance of over eight million dollars. We're in good shape."

"OK, Sis. We'll need to find a pawnshop with an employee motivated to earn some fast cash before we visit Sloan tomorrow."

CHAPTER 37

The trip from Eureka, Nevada, to the tiny community of Austin constituted seventy strenuous miles in hot, dry weather, and Carrie silently cheered when she arrived at the quaint Pony Canyon Lodge.

Based on her discussions with Hill in Ely, she suspected something would interrupt the scheduled seven-hour ride to Fallon the following day. While tomorrow promised excitement, it would not likely be physically taxing, so she relaxed on the bed with the takeout meal she'd picked up from Subway as she pedaled into town.

Austin, founded in 1862 after a Pony Express rider kicked over a quartz rock in the area and spotted silver, now reported a population of under two hundred inhabitants. A mini rush of prospectors followed the pony rider's discovery, and heavy mining operations lasted until about 1880. The population peaked in 1863 at five thousand people, then rapidly declined as the silver mines quit producing.

Today, Austin attracted tourists interested in visiting a "Living Ghost Town," representing a well-preserved example of an early Nevada mining community.

Carrie's phone showed no service bars when she attempted to contact Hill. None had been available the evening before in Eureka, either, but Carrie and Hill had spent a long session in person in Ely two nights before. They reviewed all contingencies relating to their plan during that meeting, so the inability to communicate tonight didn't present an emergency, only an annoyance. If Hill deemed personal interaction essential, he lodged in Fallon, only an hour and a half away. He could drive to Austin if he needed to.

***

When he didn't hear from her that evening, Hill tried to reach Carrie from the motel's landline. The call went to voicemail, and he left a message but suspected she wouldn't receive it. He called the number listed for the Pony Canyon Lodge, but a recorded message advised him to call back later.

Nothing had changed in the past two days except for the Brown siblings showing up in Reno unexpectedly, and Hill felt confident Carrie understood her responsibilities. Still, the sudden appearance of Brown and her brother at such a critical time troubled him. The lighted symbol on his cell phone screen confirmed Carrie had reached the lodge, so he committed to calling the motel's front desk again after dinner.

Hill walked across the street to the Golden Nugget Casino, and considered a variety of random scenarios as he ate with his bureau associate from Reno. The agent, Marina Butnari, had returned to Fallon this afternoon and would now take part in the operation until its successful completion. Both agents presumed the following busy day might offer scarce dining opportunities, so they enjoyed a big meal.

When Hill returned to his room, he removed his shoes and service holster, still thinking about the stimulating conversation with Special Agent Butnari at the restaurant. What, he wondered, were the odds of interacting with so many confident, aggressive females in such a short period? His girlfriend, his client, and now his bureau partner, all seemed more comfortable leading the dance than following.

When they'd first met several days earlier, Butnari listened intently to Hill's plan to capture Sloan. Then, she methodically suggested changes that adapted it to a better one. While her modifications created more danger for herself, they protected Carrie Brinkley infinitely better, and Hill found no flaws in her logic. Hill admitted to finding Butnari charming, but her intelligence and physique also earned his respect. At twice her size, Hill felt sure he could out-lift her, but just as confident he could not beat her in a foot race for either time or distance.

Since Butnari worked from the Reno Field Office, Hill would likely have opportunities to work with her again after his upcoming transfer. The thought made him smile, and he appreciated the coincidence responsible for her current assignment to him. Then, he remembered he didn't believe in coincidence, and an odd part of his earlier discussions with Butnari resurfaced.

When he'd mentioned he met a colleague of hers at the meetings in Greenbrier, she didn't react when he said Special Agent Sanchez's name. In fact, she changed the subject, asking Hill about how he enjoyed the special seminars presented that weekend. Perhaps her personal relationship with Sanchez was poor... or perhaps it was something else.

Before his mind could analyze the mental contradiction, something on his cell phone screen alarmed him.

By expanding the image with his fingers, he could tell the illuminated dot identifying Carrie's bicycle remained stationary in Austin. However, the symbol representing Sloan's car now moved toward Carrie's location from Fallon.

"Crap!"

He dialed Carrie's number. The call again went to voicemail, and he tried the Lodge's front desk, but received the same recorded message as earlier.

He called his agent partner in another room. "Sloan's on the move! I'm not sure when he left, but he's about halfway to Austin. Carrie has no cell service, so I'm leaving now. Meet me at the car."

As he raced for his vehicle, Hill calmed himself. He doubted Sloan would attempt something in a public location. More likely, Sloan decided to make sure Brinkley had arrived in Austin. The Ottawa Bike & Trail folks posted no update on Carrie's trip, and if Sloan tried to call the lodge, he most likely received the same recorded message Hill had. So, the only conclusive way Sloan could confirm Carrie's location was to see for himself.

That seemed logical, but Hill hated surprises. Today had already produced too many of them, and he chastised himself for not considering the possibility Sloan might begin his mission from Austin versus Fallon. The decision would likely change nothing in the plan Hill's team had discussed with Carrie, but he couldn't risk even the slim chance Sloan had a new strategy.

On top of that, the Browns now also presented a wild card in the equation.

What the hell are they up to?

***

The Pony Canyon Lodge hosted only four other overnight guests this evening. Mid-week occupancy, usually minimal, had become nonexistent many nights during the pandemic. Austin appeared on few lists as a popular tourist destination, even in the best of times.

This combination of realities caused Carrie to be concerned when the shadow of a person passed by her room at eleven o'clock at night. Light curtains covered the only window, and she wasn't sure what woke her in time to see the fleeting silhouette. She checked the integrity of the security lock on the door, and as she returned to bed, another shadow floated by the window.

A board creaked softly outside the door, and Carrie lay frozen in terror. The pounding noise in her ears frightened her, until she recognized it as the sound of her own heart. She quit breathing when an envelope slid under the door.

***

The following morning, Sloan waited across the street from the Pony Canyon Lodge. He had stationed himself next to the town's hardware store since dawn, hoping to glimpse Brinkley emerge from one of the motel's rooms.

Verifying her starting point this morning was critical to the rest of his plan for the day, but he had not risked confirming her reservation with front desk personnel the evening before. Without internet service, and with no update to the Ottawa Bike & Trail website previously, he could only count on his own eyes to confirm she stayed at the lodge.

At seven o'clock, Sloan observed Brinkley bring her bicycle through the door of a lower-level room and lean it against a post on the sidewalk. Dressed in her riding shorts and jersey, she retreated inside the room, leaving the door open.

With Brinkley's position now verified, Sloan quickly crossed the street, heading back to his vehicle. He hoped to use the town's one secondary street to intersect with Route 50 on the west side of the community ahead of Brinkley, giving her no chance to recognize his car.

Twenty minutes later, Sloan pulled to the side of the road and parked behind a grove of trees. He walked around large boulders extending over the highway to a path sloping upwards, to an elevation between some rocks. From there, he could view Route 50 in both directions, with only the portion of the road directly under the rock formation obscured.

His rifle weighed seven pounds with the scope attached, and if he held it next to his side, a passing car would not even see him carrying it.

Once situated, he removed field binoculars from a canvas bag and surveyed the geography toward the rising sun. Aided by the scope, he could see for several miles to a point where the road disappeared behind a slight bend. This morning, no cars traveled Route 50, and he had only seen one vehicle on the same stretch during all previous visits to the location.

If Brinkley left the Austin Pony Canyon Lodge soon after he'd observed her earlier, she would arrive at this spot in about an hour. Sloan set up his rifle, bracing it between two stones, then kneeled behind the rock wall and focused the binoculars on the road.

Although he'd spent the night sleeping in his compact car, Sloan felt remarkably alert. He assumed adrenalin was assisting him. This leg of Brinkley's trip represented the last and best chance to catch her on a deserted highway, and Sloan no longer had room for error. Under these circumstances, the extra precaution causing the uncomfortable evening seemed warranted.

As he waited, he anguished over the chain of events that had brought him to this place. Unlike Damien Brown, he wasn't born into crime and didn't relish the current mission. To himself, he admitted to being a coward, unable to stomach the thought of a prison sentence, and he regretted his selfishness. Though infinitely unfair, Silky Brown had dictated he trade Carrie Brinkley's life for his continued freedom.

Like it or not, that remained the deal he'd accepted. Nobody promised fairness in life, and he silently resolved this would be the last criminal act of his.

To pass the jittery minutes before Brinkley's bike would appear on the horizon, Sloan busied himself thinking about all the charitable things he would do with the money from the Pilgrim Burgers IPO. Sighing deeply, he silently wished he hadn't succumbed to the whims of a corrupt mistress.

According to his watch, the philosophical ruminations consumed only five minutes, and he searched for other things to preoccupy himself while he waited. A thought occurred to him, and he walked back to his car to retrieve a beer can from behind the front seat. After pacing to about a hundred yards, he set the empty can to the side of the road and retreated to his sniper's nest.

After peering through the binoculars in both directions, and seeing no traffic, he positioned himself with the rifle against the rock. He braced the weapon on his shoulder, found the shiny metal of the can in the scope, and concentrated on an area between the words Lone and Star. He gently applied pressure to the trigger, and his shot echoed. A split second later, the can jumped into the air.

"Perfect." The next target would be much larger than the one he just hit, and the rifle held fourteen more rounds.

Fifteen minutes passed, but time dragged in Sloan's anxious mind. He stood to urinate, then viewed the road through the binoculars again. Still no traffic. He checked his canvas bag for the third time, pulling the airline ticket from Reno to Norfolk from a zippered pocket.

The vibration of his cell phone initially startled him. He glanced at the screen, expecting the call to originate from his Vice President of

Operations in Williamsburg. Instead, the message flashed "unknown caller." Assuming it was Silky again, he pressed the "decline" option.

Seconds later, he checked voicemail for the message.

Hi, Norman. Call me back when you get this. Because of a recent change in plans, Damien and I can now assist with your current project. I'll provide more details when we speak.

"A little late, Silky," Sloan muttered, deleting the voicemail. If all went as planned today, he hoped he would never need to talk to Silky Brown again.

As the seconds crawled by, he reviewed his mental checklist. After the shot, or shots, if it took more than one, he would retrieve the shells and immediately leave the area in his car, and head west.

Though this rifle used ammunition common enough to function in various rifles, he would take no chance someone might connect a bullet from Brinkley's body to a weapon registered to him. On his way to the airport, he would deposit the empty shells and unused ammo in the Truckee River, and throw the rifle into a different stretch of it. He would tell anyone who asked that he lost the gun down a canyon when he stumbled on a steep trail while elk hunting.

Still reflecting on the fake details of the fictitious hunting expedition, Sloan viewed a single bike rider heading west through the binoculars. The bicycle, now nearly three miles in the distance, would pass within fifty yards of his hiding place, but he planned to shoot when the rider reached an area between fifty and one hundred yards away. After setting the binoculars on the rock in front of him, he raised the rifle to his cheek and found the rider in the weapon's powerful scope.

Damn!

A diesel pickup pulling a cattle carrier, heading west, passed his target on the highway. He glanced behind him, seeing no other traffic from the other direction, and hoped the cattle carrier would travel well to the west by the time he needed to take his shot. While monitoring the approaching truck through the scope, he briefly lost sight of it as it disappeared under the rock formation. The vehicle continued speeding toward Fallon when it emerged on the other side.

Relieved, Sloan reacquired the moving bicycle in the scope. Not quite a mile away, the rider, clearly a female, would take another minute to reach Sloan's preferred range. He placed the crosshairs on the biker's chest and waited for her to pedal closer.

A little more... more... OK. Three, Two —

"Remove your finger from the trigger and drop the rifle!" commanded a voice behind him. "Now, or I put a bullet in your head!"

Sloan dropped the weapon, not chancing another move.

"I am Special Agent Douglas Hill with the Federal Bureau of Investigation, and you, Norman Sloan, are under arrest for attempted murder. Please place your hands behind your back, and we'll proceed to my vehicle, where I'll read you the rest of your rights."

When they arrived at Hill's unmarked SUV parked beside Sloan's rental car, the lone female bike rider Sloan had recently targeted rolled up next to them. Sloan noticed a clear shield extending from the handlebars that had been invisible through his rifle's scope. When the rider removed her helmet, Sloan didn't recognize her.

Hill greeted the biker and tossed Sloan's rifle her way. "What do you think, Special Agent Butnari? Would a bullet from this penetrate the glass?"

The woman examined the Sig Sauer and shook her head. "Might have cracked it and given me a jolt, but that's all."

"Norman Sloan," said Hill, "meet Special Agent Marina Butnari from our Reno office. We Feds take issue with people who try to shoot our agents."

"That isn't who I expected," answered Sloan.

"Hmm," said Hill as he opened the passenger-side door to his vehicle. "Maybe you thought this person would be on the bicycle?" Carrie Brinkley exited Hill's car. "Ms. Brinkley, can you identify this man?"

"Yes, sir, that's Norman Sloan. Hi, asshole."

***

"Thank you, ma'am." Hill turned to Sloan and read the criminal his legal rights. After the brief speech, and with Brinkley and Butnari as witnesses, Hill asked, "Do you understand these rights, Mr. Sloan?"

A sullen Sloan answered, "Yes, but how did you know where I'd be, and how did you get here? The only other traffic all morning was a cattle truck."

Hill chuckled. "We aren't at liberty to discuss our methods and resources, but I rolled my vehicle out the back of the cattle carrier when we got under the rock formation here."

"Clever, but that means you knew my location."

"Oh yeah. We try to leave as little to chance as possible." Hill walked to the front of Sloan's rental car and reached beneath the bumper to retract a small, round device. "We've known where this vehicle was since it left Provo. We have assets at your other two selected sniper locations as well."

"Shit," said Sloan. "Guess I'm out of my league in the criminal department."

"You understate the obvious, Sloan, and should have taken lessons from your friend Damien Brown. Purchasing a high-powered rifle from a legitimate gun dealer causes an automatic criminal background check, which lists the seller's location. From there, we had several ways of establishing surveillance. Most crooks know that, and collect their weapons from less reputable sources."

"Damien Brown is no friend of mine—I've never met him. His sister is the one behind all this, though."

"To be clear, Mr. Sloan, nobody but you decided on this attempt. However, our government would appreciate your help to expedite justice for Sylvia Brown and her brother. We may have saved you from the death chamber by interrupting your plans for Ms. Butnari. Teresa Dill is a different story. What happened to her?"

"That was all them!" Sloan appeared frantic. "I had nothing to do with her. I don't even know where Brown is."

"Well, I can help you there," replied Hill. "They flew from Cuba yesterday to Reno, so they aren't far from here. They still have nine million dollars of your money." He paused and smiled. "Don't look so surprised. I say *your* money because you, sir, still owe the government the nine million in COVID relief funds loaned to your business."

"How did you find out about Cuba? Silky never told me where she went."

"Perhaps we can share more information with you when you share some with us, but I suspect the Browns came here because you concerned them. They'd like to make you disappear, similarly to the way Teresa Dill did."

Sloan's face lost color, and he looked around the area in sudden panic. "She called me about thirty minutes ago, but I didn't answer."

"Interesting," said Hill. "Let's get you into my car, and we'll continue our discussions on the road. We're taking you to the Northern Nevada Correctional Center in Carson City, so tell your attorney to meet us there."

"It will take my lawyer time to get here from Virginia."

"We'll wait. Special Agent Butnari, perhaps you could borrow Mr. Sloan's keys and follow us to Carson City in his rental car. Ms. Brinkley, you might prefer the company of Special Agent Butnari to Mr. Sloan and me for this trip."

CHAPTER 38

Hill led Sloan to the unmarked Bureau vehicle, which Special Agent Butnari had driven from her Reno office the day previous, as Butnari and Carrie secured the bike to a rack installed on the back. He released one of the cuffs holding Sloan's hands behind him, and clipped it to the metal bar attached to the back of the front seat. A wire cage separated front occupants from those in the back, but no other barrier interfered with conversation.

Hill pulled up the recent missed call on Sloan's cell phone, then handed the device back to Sloan.

Sloan gazed at it for a moment. "Do I gain anything by helping you with this... other than revenge with Silky?"

"I'm not an attorney, Mr. Sloan, nor a judge, so I can promise you nothing for your cooperation. However, from my point of view, you'll be in a much better position legally if we can arrest the Brown siblings. You say you had nothing to do with the disappearance of Teresa Dill. If that's the case, meaning you didn't help plan the crime, you're possibly an accessory after the fact, not an accessory before the fact."

"Talk English to me, Hill. I'm no lawyer. What's the penalty for after the fact?"

"The penalty for *before the fact* is virtually the same as for the person who commits the act. *After the fact* is significantly less. We might confirm your lessor role easier by questioning Silky and Damien."

"What if they don't talk?" asked Sloan.

"Well, we know they won't talk if they're in another country. We have many ways to encourage them to cooperate if we can control their environment in a prison cell."

"Are you talking about torture?"

"No, Sloan, we don't mistreat prisoners or use physical abuse in our country. We employ plea-bargaining, cross-examinations in which we pit the evidence provided by one criminal against that contributed by a different one, and a variety of other techniques not available to us if we can't talk to suspects directly. You should also consider the nine million dollars the Browns stole from you. Either you or your company will have to pay back those loans to the government."

"Even if I'm in jail?"

"Of course. Your obligations outside prison don't go away when you're inside, but whatever we recover from the Browns will reduce your ultimate debt. Certainly, you'll be subject to penalties for the false documents you submitted to attain the loans, but those will be lighter if you repay them. We have little chance of recovering the money if we don't capture Silky."

"OK, I'll make the call."

"Put it on speaker mode and tell her you're driving."

A moment later, Hill heard Brown answer. "Well, well, Norman. I began to worry. Where are you?"

"I didn't see the earlier call because I was up on a mountain and left my phone in the car. What do you want? I'm on my way back to Fallon."

"So, you haven't finished with Brinkley yet?"

"No, probably tomorrow, but what's it to you? You said you might help somehow in your voice message."

"That's now the case, Norman. We're not too far away from you."

"Really? When did you arrive, and why didn't you tell me you were coming?"

"Frankly, you've taken so long on the Brinkley mission, we lost confidence you could actually pull it off. I decided to help you with it so we could finally quit worrying. We flew into Reno last night. Do you want Damien's help or not?"

"Of course, I do. He has more experience at this than me."

"Good. So, what's your current plan, and where should we meet you?"

"I purchased a high-powered rifle with a scope and researched three different discrete locations along a nearly deserted highway that will work for a sniper shot. Brinkley will bike this stretch tomorrow."

"We'll need to review the maps and pick up the gun from you."

"Sure. Damien can have both. Where do you want me to drop them off?"

"We'll come to you. Tell me where you're staying."

"OK... I guess. I'll be back in about three hours. It's the Creekside Lodge in Fallon, room 133, on the first floor. I'll park my rental car in front of the room. It's a red Focus."

"We'll find it. See you later."

After the call ended, Sloan handed his mobile phone to Hill in the front seat. "She didn't even ask about the locations I selected."

"I doubt she ever planned to use them."

"Guess not. What now? You stick me in the motel room for bait?"

"No. Special Agent Butnari and I will switch cars up here. You'll go to Carson City with her, and I'll take your car to the Creekside Lodge."

"What if she's watching for me when this car gets there?"

"You told her you'd arrive back in Fallon in three hours, but I'll get there in forty-five minutes. I doubt she'd set up surveillance that early, but if she does, she'll observe a man about your size exit the Focus and enter the room. She'll never see my face."

***

Carrie and Butnari had driven in silence, each absorbed in thought until Butnari received the call from Hill, driving the Bureau car behind them.

"New development," said Butnari as she pulled to the side of the road. "Silky Brown just spoke with Sloan, and she wants to meet him at his motel. We'll switch and take the Bureau car to Carson City with Sloan, and Special Agent Hill will take Sloan's rental back to the Creekside Lodge in Fallon. Sorry for the extra company. Will you be OK with Sloan riding in the back?"

"No problem at all. He's the one who'll feel uncomfortable. I have over a month's worth of bad vibes to send him."

"Great!" Butnari laughed. "I'll muster some up as well. Poor guy."

***

"Got him!" announced Silky to Damien. "That was Sloan. He's out reviewing sniper locations but will return to his motel in a few hours."

"So, he's done nothing yet?"

"No. He planned to use a rifle on Brinkley tomorrow, and I suggested you had more experience in things like that. He seemed glad to relinquish the role."

"But we won't worry about Brinkley anymore, right?"

"Right, and now I'm sorry I bullied Sloan into chasing her all over the country. He's an incompetent criminal with more potential to get caught in the act of a crime than to commit one successfully. If the police catch him, he's going to jail anyway and will have no incentive to stay quiet about us."

"OK. I have a thirty-eight caliber with no serial number and a lead pipe from the pawnshop. What time do you want to leave?"

"It will take about an hour to get to Fallon from here, and I'd like to be at his motel early enough to monitor the parking lot for a while. Let's take off at two o'clock. Better get a nap because we'll drive most of the night when we finish with Sloan. I want to be south of Los Angeles by dawn."

***

Damien drove to Fallon, and Silky immediately spotted the Focus when they entered the parking lot of the Creekside Lodge.

"Park by the dumpster," she instructed her brother.

The couple monitored the premises from their car for forty-five minutes before easing the Jeep to a spot near the red Focus.

A lone cleaning cart sat in front of an open door to a room four doors from Sloan's on the otherwise vacant sidewalk. After a last peek around, Silky and Damien left their car to approach room 133.

Silky knocked on the door three times, but nobody answered. She raised her arm to try again, but the door opened, revealing a tall man with a handgun on the other side.

***

"You must be Sylvia Brown," Hill said. "Damien, don't move your arm another millimeter, or you'll die from three different bullets. Look to either side of you."

To Damien's left, a female officer in a hospitality staff uniform stood beside the cleaning cart, her legs spread in a shooting stance with a pistol aimed directly at Damien's head

A fit young man now appeared in the open doorway of the adjacent room to the right, also holding a revolver pointed at Damien.

Hill reached across the entry and removed the thirty-eight from Damien's trouser pocket. "Both of you place your hands behind you, and we'll proceed inside for other formalities."

CHAPTER 39

The three-hour drive to Carson City would knock off four days of bicycling for Carrie, and she found herself enjoying Special Agent Butnari's company. Only two years older than Carrie, Butnari—*'Please call me Marina'*—displayed the physique of a competitive beach volleyball player and the wit of a stand-up comedian.

Once they switched cars, Butnari actuated the glass sound barrier separating the front and back seats so that she and Carrie could talk.

Carrie said, "Agent Hill is lucky I wasn't carrying a gun last night when he put the envelope under my door."

"You were awake when that happened? Doug thought you might be asleep but hoped you'd see the note when you got up. I'm sorry it scared you, but he didn't want to hang around too long, for obvious reasons."

"I understand, but I couldn't sleep and glimpsed his shadow in the window. Where did Sloan stay last night?"

"In his car. We found the Focus about three blocks away from the motel when we arrived. I drove past it with Doug and parked behind a truck on the next street. He left the car for a little while around dusk, and when he returned, he reclined the front seat all the way back. We took turns monitoring his vehicle but didn't see him again until he got out of the car this morning."

"Oh my God, Marina! You must be exhausted if you stayed up all night."

"No. As I said, we took shifts. Doug would watch for two hours while I slept, then we'd switch. Around 11:00, we decided Sloan was down for the night, so Doug snuck up to your room with the envelope outlining the new plan. We thought Sloan might leave his car early to verify when you left the motel."

"Which is pretty much what happened."

"Close. Doug followed Sloan at dawn and tracked him to the corner of the store across from the motel. When Sloan saw you bring your bike outside the room, he returned to his car and drove away. He just needed to ensure you had stayed there, and probably feared you might remember the Focus from the Monarch Pass incident, if he passed you on Route 50. So, he took off ahead of you."

"Which allowed you to take my bike at the motel rather than someplace on the road."

Marina nodded. "Right. I needed the extra exercise, and wanted you to get to know Doug better."

Carrie stared over at her driver, and Marina burst into a laugh. "Come on, Carrie! I'm joking."

"Of course!" Carrie lied. "Agent Hill and I did spend a lot of time talking over the last three weeks, but I can't say I got to know him well. He's a decent person, and an excellent agent from my vantage point, but he's mysterious."

Butnari glanced sideways at her passenger. "I noticed the same thing when I came out to collaborate with him last week. So, when I got back to Reno last week, I did a little research."

"Are you interested in him?" Carrie asked innocently.

"No... no. Nothing like that, but we agents like to understand a little about the people we partner with on dangerous cases. Hill comes from the Criminal Justice Information Services Division in West Virginia, where he has a desk job. Nobody here ever heard of him until recently, and the Bureau rarely gives desk jockeys field assignments."

Butnari didn't continue, and Carrie asked, "Is that it?"

"No, he's more interesting than that. He performed like a young super-star field agent in Baltimore before he ended up in rehab for alcohol. Lost his wife and nearly his job. Out of the recovery center, the Bureau sent him to West Virginia, and he'll transfer from there soon. People up the chain of command in the agency think he's too valuable to keep on the bench in West Virginia."

"Aww... good for him! So, his success with this case won't hurt him any."

"Not at all. It may help in a variety of ways," Butnari added cryptically. "Would you like to know some other things about the man responsible for saving your life?"

"Of course. Sounds like you researched him rather thoroughly."

"Professional curiosity comes with the job, and Hill isn't aware I know what I'm going to tell you. I'm not breaking any rules by sharing with you, and you could find the same things in public records if you looked hard enough. I find his background fascinating, but can we keep this between us?"

"Certainly, Marina. Thank you."

"He received his GED at a Correctional Center in Kentucky after landing there as a junior in high school. According to court files, he sent another student to the hospital because of a fight."

"No! That doesn't seem possible. He's such a gentle, even-keeled person. Did you find out what happened?"

"Duh! I investigate for a living. Doug witnessed a kid soak a stray cat in gasoline, then set the animal on fire. The boy laughed as the tortured animal ran in circles until it died. Hill saw the whole thing from an adjacent yard but couldn't get to the cat in time to help it, so he confronted the bully. They settled the disagreement with fists, and three other neighborhood youths had to pull Doug away. After doctors treated the kid at the hospital for some cuts, his father, a local politician, convinced a judge to place Doug in the Fayette Juvenile Detention Center."

"Wow. Seems like an extreme punishment for a front-yard fistfight, but Hill seems like my kind of criminal."

"Right," said Butnari. "Mine too."

Agents met their car in Carson City to retrieve Sloan, and Butnari drove Carrie to the Circus Circus Casino & Hotel in Reno, where the government had secured accommodations for her.

CHAPTER 40

After completing the paperwork required to book the Brown siblings into temporary cell accommodations at the Northern Nevada Correctional Center, Hill found Special Agent Butnari waiting for him in the lobby.

"Good work, Doug."

"Thank you for your help, Marina. We made a pretty solid team."

"I was thinking the same thing. I dropped Carrie off at the Circus Circus in Reno, and she understands she'll need to attend the debriefing with you tomorrow. You can make arrangements to pick her up. I invited her to stay with me for an evening, after your meetings, before she resumes her bike trip."

"That's nice of you. Do you think the local office will allow her to continue to California before the arraignments next week?"

"They don't want to, but I thought of an alternate plan they might accept. We don't need Carrie at the arraignments, so her safety is the only reason to keep her in Reno. I might have a way to do that without confining her here. When do you return to West Virginia?"

"Probably after the meeting tomorrow."

"Should I get you a room at the Circus Circus for the night? That would make retrieving Carrie in the morning more convenient."

"I still need to check out of the room and collect my things in Fallon, so I might as well stay there this evening. It's a short ride to Reno, and getting Carrie won't be a problem. I'll book a late afternoon flight back to West Virginia."

"Do you know the time for the flight?"

"There's one at four o'clock that connects in Chicago. Why?"

"Our office here reports to District Headquarters in Las Vegas, and the Special Agent in Charge there, Russell Coles, has an interest in meeting you."

"Sure. I'll look forward to that when I come back. I can't make it to Vegas on this trip, but I'll be here next week for the arraignment. Is the meeting about this case?"

"Among other things, but I should leave that for Special Agent Coles to discuss. Like most of us in this business, he has little patience and doesn't need it in his position. He's planning to fly up tomorrow to visit with you at our Reno office. Would that present a problem?"

Hill laughed. "You're funny, Marina. When the head of one of our district headquarters requests a personal meeting with an agent, the agent better not have a problem with it. The briefing at your offices starts at ten and shouldn't take more than an hour. What time do you think Coles will arrive from Vegas?"

"He has access to an agency Gulfstream, so he'll be here by eight."

"Of course, he would want his meeting ahead of the other one. Great. Then an afternoon flight back to West Virginia should work—unless you disagree."

"No. That sounds fine. We'll finish our meeting with Coles early, and I don't think the briefing session relating to Sloan will last long."

"You said '*our* meeting with Coles.' Will you attend that one, too?"

Butnari smiled. "Yes, I'm the reason for it."

"What am I missing here, Marina?"

"How much do you know about your next assignment after CJIS?"

"Hardly anything, except it's so secret few are aware I even have a new assignment. How did you know about it?"

"Because my code name is Angel."

Hill absorbed the bombshell quietly and without emotion, never unlocking his eyes from Butnari's. After several moments, he asked, "So, Special Agent Coles is Bluntforce?"

"I can't answer that question, but I'd like to welcome you officially to Operation Night Landing."

"Thank you, Marina. I guess I'll work for you then?"

"No, you'll work *with* me. I'm just the team leader for our unit. I don't mean to sound mysterious, but I can share more with you tomorrow after our talk with Coles. We'll have plenty of time before your flight."

"I understand, but before you go, could you answer something else for me?"

"I will if I'm allowed to, Doug. What is it?"

"Was the fact that you worked with me on this case a coincidence?"

"Do you believe in coincidences?"

"No."

"Neither do I."

"Thank you, Marina. I'll see you in the morning."

CHAPTER 41

The following day, Hill picked Carrie up at the hotel lobby. On the way to the briefing, he shared the details of his arrest of Damien and Silky.

"Wow!" said Carrie. "Is that like a bonus? If the Browns blackmailed Sloan to eliminate me, what made it so important for them to come here to assist him?"

"They weren't here to help Sloan. Brown's plan to remain in Cuba fell apart, and Sloan became a bigger liability to them than you. They came to silence Sloan, and we just got lucky. They carried a suitcase in their vehicle with nearly $500,000 in cash, and I believe they'd have slipped over the Mexican border by sometime today."

"Are they talking? Did they admit to killing Teresa?"

"No. They're both smarter criminals than Sloan. They won't talk until their legal representation arrives, but they're in secure cells with no hope of bail. Sloan provided us with enough evidence to hold them indefinitely. His attorney gets here this evening, but that hasn't kept Sloan from sharing. He became extremely cooperative when he realized how close he came to being murdered by the Browns."

"Well, thank you, Doug... for protecting me and for your patience."

"You're welcome, Carrie. I enjoyed working with you. You're a courageous woman with inspirational determination."

Hill expected little to happen on the case until after Sloan and the Browns met with counsel, so he planned to return to West Virginia. Sloan's arraignment at the Federal Court in Reno would take place the following week, and he would be back for that.

He agreed to keep Carrie apprised, and promised she was in excellent hands with Special Agent Butnari.

***

Marina picked Carrie up from the Circus Circus, and the two spent the evening at the agent's townhouse. Carrie called her parents, Ottawa

Bike & Trail, and Russ Dennison from Marina's residence. She attempted to minimize the drama of recent events, but the conversation with her parents lasted over an hour. Hal threatened to book a flight to Reno that evening, but Carrie told him about her new roommate's occupation as an FBI agent. The announcement took the steam out of the argument, and Carrie promised to call every evening until she arrived in Mendocino.

Carrie's tale shocked Jeff Carroll and his brother, but they agreed nobody would benefit by sensationalizing the criminal activities associated with the journey. Carrie would double-down on pictures as she passed through Napa, and Jeff planned to meet her in Mendocino. The mayor of the small community had already contacted Jeff about scheduling an event around the time of Carrie's arrival in the seacoast town. A representative from Piker would also attend the function.

The conversation with Russ didn't go as well, and Marina politely left the room to allow Carrie to speak privately.

***

"What do you mean somebody had plans to assassinate you? When did all that start, and why?"

Carrie sighed. "It had something to do with a fraud my old boss and his girlfriend attempted at the company where I used to work. They thought I possessed incriminating evidence about what they were doing."

"Why didn't you tell me this in Ottawa? Was the accident here an attempt on your life?"

"Yes, Russ, but I didn't realize it then. I also understood nothing about what my former boss was attempting with my old company."

"So, when did you find out?"

"Not for sure until Colorado, when another car tried to run me off the road. At that point, I called a law enforcement contact I established back in Ottawa, and we started piecing things together."

"Carrie, we've talked almost every evening of your trip. It isn't like you had no opportunities to share this with me. What's going on?"

"Nothing, Russ. I just didn't want to worry you, and once an FBI agent started protecting me around the clock, I was in little danger."

"Not the point, Carrie," said an exasperated Russ. "I'm glad you're safe and that the man who was stalking you is in jail. It's just... I care about you so much that I feel the right to know when I need to worry about you. You disagree and don't understand why I think it's a big deal.

I'm not sure what else to say except that you've left me out of something important, and I'm struggling to reconcile that."

"Russ, I'm sorry you feel like this, and it isn't what I intended."

"Maybe not, Carrie, but we both have things to consider. Thanks for calling, and we'll talk again after your trip. Enjoy the rest of your ride." Then he hung up.

***

As Carrie sat alone in the den after the call, Marina joined her on the sofa. "That didn't sound so pleasant."

"It wasn't," said Carrie. "He's angry because I didn't confide in him about the danger I encountered during the trip since Ottawa."

"I've never met Russ and barely know you, Carrie, but when you disappoint a man because you didn't give him a chance to worry about you properly... that's the sort of man I'd like to have around."

Carrie stopped sniffling and focused on her new friend. Tears had given way to a flame burning deep in her eyes. "You're right, and I *do* want Russ around. I made a mistake, but it isn't my first one. I'm going to fix it."

"Will you call him back?"

"Nope. I'm going to take a job with Ottawa Bike & Trail at the end of this bicycle trip and live in his hometown. I'll hound him until he allows me the opportunity to make even more mistakes, and until he realizes mistakes are part of the deal! You don't give up after them. You fix 'em and move on. I'm probably going to marry that man."

"Whoa! That's an aggressive plan. Have you always been this way?"

"No." Carrie chuckled. "It seems to be a recent development."

"Well, I think it's a good one. Congratulations, but can I ask you a personal question?"

"Certainly, but do I need more wine?"

"No, and I don't want to throw cold water on your plan, but do you really want to live in Kansas? It isn't like either Virginia or California."

Carrie stared at her new friend without answering, her mind in another place.

"I'm sorry," Marina finally said. "I haven't been any place in Kansas besides the airport. What do I know? I didn't mean to upset you."

At last, snapping out of her daze, Carrie said, "No... no, Marina. I'm not upset. What you said reminded me of something my father told me before I started the trip. I didn't think much about it at the time... but now... I suddenly realize how right he was!"

"OK, so are you going to tell me? What was your father right about?"

"Yes, but now I *do* need more wine."

Marina refreshed Carrie's glass with the Russian River Chardonnay they had been drinking, and Carrie continued. "Just before I started my bike trip — one reason for it — my boyfriend decided to break up with me and return to Alabama. Trey was an 'Adonis' — a big, strong, professional baseball player who hit home runs for a living, and he had the most charming southern accent. I thought I loved him, but I'm pretty sure now I might have just loved his body. He definitely loved mine."

"So, why didn't you go with him? Your boss had already fired you, right?"

"Yes, but I didn't want to move to Alabama. When I told my dad Trey left me, he corrected me and said I *allowed* Trey to leave, that I didn't lose him — he lost me. He pointed out that when the right guy came along, it wouldn't matter to me where I lived. Now, he seems the smartest man in the world because I don't care where Russ lives. I want to be in the same place."

"So, you're sure Russ is the 'right guy' your dad talked about?"

"No, but I'm sure he's close, and I'm looking forward to conducting some additional research."

"Let's have some more wine."

***

After dinner, Marina clinked wine glasses with Carrie. "I have a proposal for you, which I hope you'll consider."

"I'm listening. As long as it doesn't interfere with finishing this trip, I'm interested."

"It doesn't. You *should* finish it, but I wondered if you might like some company for the rest of the way."

"What do you mean? Does the FBI want to escort me now?"

"The Bureau wouldn't mind that. Nobody believes you're in further danger with Sloan and the Browns behind bars, but you're an important witness in a complicated case. We have a significant investment in you with compelling reasons to protect it."

"I understand," said Carrie, "but assigning an agent to ride the rest of my journey with me would run the government tab up even more."

"Right. Therefore, the Bureau would prefer you stay in a safe place in Reno until after we officially arraign Sloan and the Browns."

Carrie reacted, and Marina held up a hand. "I guessed that option wouldn't charm you and suggested a different approach. When Special Agent Hill's supervisor contacted our office last week, my boss had several reasons to assign me to the case. It helped that we're about the same age with similar builds, but I'm also an avid biker. I've wanted to bike across the mountains to the Pacific for years, and I volunteered to take a week of vacation to go with you. The Bureau allowed the trip without requiring vacation time."

"I'd love a companion, Marina! I estimated the rest of the journey would take about six days from Reno to Mendocino, but we don't have to go that fast. I don't mind slowing down from here."

"My preferred fitness routine is biking, and I ride four miles up a mountain near here three times per week. I can keep up with you."

"Great! The route from here is not only scenic, but we also ride through wine country."

"I'm aware," said Butnari. "That's my other favorite fitness routine— wine drinking. I might hold us up for an evening when we get to the wine-tasting part."

"Perfect! I'm excited. A company in Kansas sponsors my trip, so you can stay with me in motels along the way. I also carry everything we need in my pack for emergency repairs and things."

"No problem, but the Bureau will cover my expenses. We can stay in more expensive motels than the Super 8, and I have tools too. I pack safety equipment much more effective than pepper spray."

"Of course, you would," said Carrie with a wink.

CHAPTER 42

The flight back to Morgantown took three hours, which felt more like fifteen minutes. Hill's mental efforts to consider, categorize, and catalog the flood of information accumulated in the past twenty-four hours made the trip from Reno pass quickly.

In the morning meeting with the agent in charge of the Las Vegas Field Office, Hill learned Coles managed many resources required for Operation Night Landing. He wasn't Bluntforce, however, and Coles made it clear that participants on the task force had no "need to know" the identity of whoever was. Hill wondered if Coles himself even had that information.

If Operation Night Landing was managed from Coles' field office, Hill thought it unlikely the man wouldn't be fully apprised of all resources allocated to it. He remembered the intensity of his conversations with Coles' second-in-command, Special Agent Alice Harbison, when the two had met at the Greenbrier Resort. Not that it mattered, but Hill concluded he had a good idea of Bluntforce's identity.

Marina, now known to him as "Angel," shared as much as she could, which was enough to excite Hill about the job. The operation would involve initiatives to affect worldwide human trafficking, and his team would collaborate with covert operatives from at least six other enforcement organizations. As he had guessed, the enigmatic pastor, Tom Burns, would also play a role in the mission.

After the debriefing meeting on the Sloan case, Marina had driven Hill to a nearby restaurant for lunch, and shared some of her unique history.

***

She arrived in the United States five years earlier from Moldova as part of a trio of young women trafficked by a sinister Asian criminal organization. Rescued in a dramatic interdiction conducted at the Dulles Airport, she received a T-Visa to remain in the States.

Pastor Tom Burns had facilitated the rescue, then coordinated an effort enabling Marina to finish her college studies, begun at Moldova University, at Florida International University. After attaining a degree, the FBI accepted Marina for training at their National Academy in Quantico. She finished the course academically at the top of her class, then further distinguished herself in the traditional final physical challenge. A grueling obstacle course had replaced the legendary Yellow Brick Road as the Academy's final check mark for graduation, and Marina set a record on it.

Now, she would lead a selected team of trained agents to mitigate the horrific crime she had nearly fallen victim to. She refused to discuss the nature of her current relationship with Pastor Burns, stipulating security reasons, but laughed at Hill's recollections of the minister from the two poker games. She said her assignment to assist Hill with Sloan had been a lucky and timely opportunity to engage with her potential new partner in action, and she'd enthusiastically accepted it. After confirming to him he hadn't disappointed her, Marina surprised Hill by inquiring about Henrietta Mendoza.

"What about her?" asked Hill. "You did some deep research to come up with that name."

"We're both professional investigators, Doug. Your connection to her didn't take exceptional skills to uncover. Do you believe she may join you in Nevada?"

"Would it make a difference to the job offer?"

"Not now. You're already selected. If you had been married when we began profiling candidates for the position, Bluntforce might not have considered you."

"Why?"

"The ruthless criminals involved with trafficking deploy sadistic tactics against the families and loved ones of agents they wish to compromise. We try to protect these innocents and our team members by recruiting unit members with more limited personal ties."

"To answer your first question, I don't know. I care for Ms. Mendoza but don't believe she'll give up her career to move west."

"I'm sorry to hear that, Doug. The reports about her show she's a remarkable lady."

"She is, but from what you told me, she might pose a liability to your operation if she moved."

"Not so much. Her training as a police officer equips her to handle the risks involved in law enforcement, and to understand the importance of confidentiality. You are more experienced than me, but I find that agents with healthy personal lives balance a demanding professional one better. I wish you success in convincing Mendoza to join you out here."

***

The jolt and slight squeal from the wheels as they touched the tarmac in Morgantown interrupted Hill's reflection. After glancing at the long list of things he needed to do, compiled during the flight, he expected the next several days at CJIS to be busy. However, he hoped he might schedule a quick trip to Baltimore before returning to Reno for Sloan's arraignment.

CHAPTER 43

The entire journey across the country had been an epic adventure for Carrie, but the part between Reno and Mendocino created a different kind of memory she'd cherish for life. Originally planned as a five-day segment of her trip, Napa became a week-long excursion with her new friend, Special Agent Marina Butnari.

The biking from Reno to Auburn, California, provided strenuous exercise, but with Marina, Carrie stopped more often to enjoy the spectacular vistas along the way. Marina also enjoyed the pauses, but not because she needed to rest. The agent's physical fitness surpassed Carrie's, and the bike activity didn't challenge her. The shared experiences, punctuated with wine tasting, caused a professional relationship to grow into a genuine friendship.

One evening, Carrie asked her friend, "When did Doug figure out that Damien Brown killed Teresa? His sister, Silky, worked at Pilgrim Burgers with me, but we weren't friends. Are you allowed to share that?"

"Probably not, but I trust you. We got lucky after Sloan purchased the rifle and Doug received the alert resulting from the background check. Damien Brown's car surfaced on a suspected abandoned vehicle list posted by the Kansas City airport. Virginia tags on a deserted car in Kansas, cross-referenced with data relating to your accident in Ottawa, created another CJIS alert to Doug. He processed the tags and registration and then tried to contact Brown, who had fled the country with his sister. Brown's long criminal history accounts for plenty of information on him in the database, and Doug easily connected his relationship to Silky."

"So, after Silky's brother tried to kill me, he left his car at the airport and took off?"

"Yep. When Doug attempted to reach Silky at Pilgrim Burgers, a receptionist told him she was vacationing. He checked airline reservations from Norfolk under her name and discovered a Southwest flight to Havana through Miami, which also listed her brother. No fake IDs — they traveled on legitimate passports under their real names."

"So, what made me important to them? I called the Missing Persons Hotline and told the officer my suspicions about the COVID money fraud, but I had nothing very incriminating."

"Frankly, Carrie, Brown and Sloan made a huge mistake there. You presented a minor threat to their strategy, and they over-reacted in the efforts to eliminate you. The plan may have succeeded if they hadn't been so aggressive."

"Because the evidence I gave the hotline was so weak?" asked Carrie.

"Don't scold yourself. You provided the first clue about the disappearance of Teresa Dill, but your information wasn't sufficient to warrant subpoenas or further investigation. Teresa Dill represented a dead-end missing persons case, and we had no proof of fraud against Sloan."

"But then the connection between Damien Brown's car and my accident made Doug suspicious?"

"Yes. He kept your report to the Newport News police on his desk at CJIS, and placed your name in the Bureau's database. The accident in Kansas created an alert that went to his desk."

"Then Sloan's amateur attempts to finish what Damien couldn't unraveled Silky Brown's perfect plan."

"I think so," said Marina. "Without Sloan's testimony against her, we may not have ever known where to instruct authorities to look for her body."

***

The extra evenings spent in St. Helena and Cloverdale related to wine-drinking more than biking. The distance scheduled for this segment totaled only about fifty miles, but Carrie and Marina accumulated dozens of additional miles each day visiting the vineyards of the Napa region.

In Cloverdale, on the last evening before heading for the coast, the two women discussed the following day's plan. Carrie wanted Marina to accompany her to the Pacific Ocean in Mendocino, but the agent insisted on dropping back behind Carrie as the couple approached the scenic oceanfront community.

"Two reasons," said Marina. "One, this journey is yours, and you should complete it as you started it — alone. Second, your trip is a unique accomplishment during the pandemic crisis, and the FBI escorting you to the finish line should not confuse its importance. Achieving your mission should send a message of commitment, resilience, and hope to all who follow it. Let's not do anything to dilute that."

"OK. I see your point, but what I did wasn't such an earth-shattering deal. I'm not the first to bicycle across America, and won't be the last."

"Correct, but you're one of only a few who did it this year, when we needed the distraction, and something uncontroversial to cheer for."

"I understand, and we'll do it your way, but can I ask you a question?"

"Sure."

"Will you do it with me again sometime? I enjoyed this past week so much I forgot your part was a professional obligation."

"Carrie, the trip became personal after the first four hours. I'd love another biking adventure like this, and if we can't take off for two months for a long one, I bet you'll have a list of shorter ones in the Midwest."

"Deal," said Carrie, forgetting the COVID crisis momentarily to give her friend a warm hug. "So, lady, you're aware of my plans after Mendocino. After a few days there, I head to Ottawa, Kansas. My parents don't even know that yet! Your plans seem more mysterious, or do you just not share them with me? What's up with Doug?"

Marina chuckled and relaxed back into her chair. "Mmm, I don't have a lot to share, Carrie. My course from here isn't a secret, but the timing and details of what happens in my career are not entirely determined. I think you heard that our Reno office offered Doug a new assignment in our district, and he's joining us in a couple of months. I look forward to working with him."

Carrie laughed. "Is that all?"

"What do you mean?"

"When we talked in the car after Sloan's attempted ambush, your interest in Doug seemed to go beyond his abilities as a fellow agent on my case. You researched his personal life fairly thoroughly."

Marina smiled and sipped her wine. "I'm sorry I gave you the wrong impression, Carrie. We're new friends, and there's much you don't know about me. As you correctly surmised, my reasons for checking him out had little to do with you or Sloan, but they were professional, not personal."

"I'm sorry, Marina, and embarrassed I presumed a romantic interest."

"Don't be. Doug is a big ole country boy from Kentucky with a beautiful heart. Also, a fine-looking man, but not my type. I like that he's a veteran who's endured unfortunate breaks, made a few mistakes, weathered some storms, and not some shiny quarter fresh out of the mint. He'll be an excellent associate."

CHAPTER 44

When Hill arrived at his office in West Virginia, two messages from the Norfolk Field Office, and one from Special Agent Butnari, awaited him. The first voicemail indicated the Virginia Marine Police had agreed to drag the Elizabeth River, and the second informed Hill the Federal District Court in Norfolk granted subpoenas for agents to search all Pilgrim Burgers' receipts for the past three months. Butnari's message only asked him to call her for an update.

As he reached for his desk phone, Jim Strong took a seat in front of him. "Congratulations, Doug! Looks like you'll leave our humble outpost on a high note. You solved one murder, prevented another, and I suspect we'll recover most of the money the Browns stole."

"We're not there yet, Jim, but somebody did a boatload of work while I flew from Reno yesterday. Thanks. Do you know if the Browns started talking?"

"No. Their attorney will arrive in Reno today, but Sloan didn't wait for his. He's desperate to avoid the murder rap, and he asked to speak to either you or your friend, Special Agent Butnari, yesterday afternoon."

"So, what did he give Butnari?"

"Silky Brown sent Sloan a text message detailing the location of Dill's body with a jpeg attached showing a receipt from Lowe's. Sloan's signature appeared on the receipt. Brown provided Sloan with the information as proof she could also send the same information to others. The text represented a key part of her blackmail scheme to induce Sloan to murder Brinkley."

"Did you check his cell phone to confirm the text?"

"No, because he told Butnari he had already deleted it. But he remembered from Brown's message the approximate spot in the river her brother dropped Dill's body, and the exact amount of the Lowe's receipt—$167.50 for a logging chain, bolt-cutter, and handcart, which he thought divers would find with or near the body."

"If he signed the receipt, why would he incriminate himself by providing the information?"

"He says he didn't sign it. Brown forged his name."

"Interesting. So, if we can match Brown's handwriting to the signature, we can connect her to the murder."

"Right. We don't think she performed the act. Most likely, Damien did that, but if we find the things bought from Lowes near the body, we can establish her involvement. Circumstantially, discovery will prove she stole nine million dollars and fled the country to Cuba. Makes her look pretty guilty."

"What about Sloan?" asked Hill.

"This is your case, Doug, but I believe what Sloan told Butnari. We recorded the conversation, by the way. He says Brown didn't apprise him of her plan for Dill, only that she would take care of the problem. Sloan and Brown conspired to embezzle the COVID relief money, and Brown feared Dill planned to expose them. It will irritate his attorney when he finds out everything Sloan told us without him present, but he'll probably make a decent case for accessory after the fact."

"Thanks, Jim. I'd better call Norfolk and see how they're doing."

***

When Hill returned Marina's call, she updated him on her conversation with Sloan, providing little more detail than what Strong shared earlier. He briefed her on what he knew about the police activities occurring in Tidewater.

Late in the day, the Norfolk office called Hill with news that the Virginia Marine Police recovered the body of a female, or what was left of it, from the Elizabeth River. The torso, still wrapped in a carpet secured by a logging chain, remained mainly intact. The police boat didn't find bolt cutters but pulled up a handcart that lay next to the submerged body. Authorities believed identification of the deceased seemed likely, but perhaps not the definite cause of the death. Agents found no receipt for $167.50 at the Pilgrim Burgers office, but the company's bank provided a photocopy of a similar charge from their records. Norman Sloan's signature on the receipt matched many others on company disbursements, but several employees verified that Sloan regularly allowed Silky Brown to sign his name for weekly payments to vendors. Hill felt confident a forensic document examiner would confirm that Silky signed the Lowe's receipt.

Hill doubted Silky would implicate her brother. Based on the evidence, however, a jury would almost certainly convict Damien of capital murder. Before the current year, that would have put him on death row, but Virginia had recently abolished capital punishment. Now, Damien would most likely serve a life sentence with no possibility of parole. Silky would earn sentences for several crimes, the most serious an accessory before the fact to murder.

With a sharp attorney, Sloan might slide by with only the accessory after the fact murder charge and depart prison in less than five years. Hill had interrupted Sloan's plan for the more serious premeditated capital murder of Carrie Brinkley, but the agent didn't expect any gratitude from Sloan.

***

Hill's visit with Henrietta in Baltimore transpired perfectly — dampened only by the shadow of their impending separation. The Orioles won a rare game with the Yankees at Camden Yards in the pandemic-shortened season, and the crabs at Bo Brooks afterward were legendary. They watched the sun dip below the western horizon from a bench at the Inner Harbor, neither willing to raise the unanswered question that hung between them.

When they returned to Henri's Federal Point condominium after the nearly perfect day, Doug reluctantly resolved to accept Henri's reticence as her answer. Respectful of her circumstances and appreciative of her past support, he could ask nothing more from her.

Until he saw the brochure for High Sierra Security next to the TV in Henri's bedroom.

"What's this, Henri?"

"Oh, nothing really. Just something I received in the mail," replied Henri as she returned from the vanity.

"Information relating to a business near Reno isn't 'nothing'! Why didn't you tell me you still considered a move west?"

"Doug, I know you too well. When you find a single clue, you think you solved the case, and I'm doing my best to control your expectations. You and our relationship *are* important to me, and I'm not sure of the right decision. Every possibility deserves careful reflection, though, and I'm just trying to gather all the relevant data."

"Well, you've now successfully revived my hopes. Can you tell me about High Sierra Security?"

"The company offers guard and protection services for several large corporations in Nevada and California. They also earned Department of

Defense contracts for several regional military installations. It's a private company owned by a former four-star United States Marine Corps general, and they only hire people with law enforcement backgrounds. The Baltimore Police Force qualifies in that category."

"So, you talked to someone there?"

"See, you're getting excited, and I don't want that yet. I have a lot of research to do, but I spoke with the company's Chief of Staff. She didn't need much information from me when she returned my phone call because she had already prepared a file on me. Sort of scary, frankly. I can't guess her source, but the details were accurate."

"Do you think they would hire you?"

"I know they would. She made an offer. Their starting package, not negotiable, doesn't change for anyone."

"How's the money?"

"Less than what I currently make to start, but the benefits are excellent, the hours better, and the firm offers opportunities to earn additional bonus income."

"What do you think?"

"That I need to think," said Henri, smiling. "I'm not overly concerned by the pay cut because I'm pretty sure I can reduce my overall living expenses with a roommate out there. But... I've put ten years of hard work in here, and the force has me on a fast track to promotion. Starting all over with Sierra makes me anxious."

"I understand, but you know my vote—and don't worry about the roommate. I won't bug you about it anymore, Henri, but thank you for considering."

Henrietta gazed at Doug for a long moment before shaking her head and sighing. "Someday, our kids are gonna get a good laugh about how we met."

"Kids?"

"Close your mouth, Doug, and get in bed."

CHAPTER 45

Carrie and Marina left Navarro, California, at 9 AM for the last four-hour leg of Carrie's cross-country journey, after concluding their extended exploration of the Napa Valley region. They expected a triumphant arrival in Mendocino, and Carrie rode several miles in deep thought next to her new friend. Then she suddenly noticed the stunning scenery surrounding her. Trees—giant trees—rose hundreds of feet on both sides of the road, sometimes blocking out the sky.

California State Route 128 snaked through the Navarro River Redwoods State Park on its way to connect with the Pacific Ocean, and Carrie found the ride spellbinding. After motioning Marina to pull off the highway near some picnic tables, Carrie leaned her bicycle against one and removed her helmet.

"Are you OK?" asked Marina.

"I'm fine, just overwhelmed by these magnificent trees. When Woodie Guthrie sang about *the redwood forest to the Gulf Stream waters*, I never imagined this!"

"They're amazing, aren't they? Unless you see them, you can't fully appreciate their majesty. Many of these trees pre-date Christ, and the oldest one, located north of here, is over three thousand years old."

The young women remained quiet for several minutes, each privately contemplating the beauty and tranquility of the sanctuary created beneath the canopy of some of the planet's oldest living things.

Finally, Carrie left her place by the bike and walked to where Marina stood. Saying nothing, she embraced her friend, holding her tight with both arms. "Thank you, Marina... for so many things, but mostly, thank you for being here to enjoy this awesome moment with me."

Marina held back a trace of mist in her eyes. "Thank *you*, Carrie. I will *never* forget this moment."

With no other words necessary, Carrie returned to her bike.

Marina said, "When we hit Route 1 at the Pacific, I'll drop about a mile behind you. We'll still have several miles to go, but I want to make sure everyone sees you enter Mendocino alone."

"Got it."

***

When Carrie arrived at the outskirts of the quaint ocean-front community a little after two o'clock, her agent friend slowed and disappeared behind. A banner hanging over the highway read, "Welcome, Carrie Brinkley! Follow the purple ribbons."

A TV news helicopter hovering above her explained how people in the town knew her arrival time. Smiling citizens lined her route, waving as she wound down toward the Russian Gulch State Park beach. A van displaying the call letters for the local TV station fell in behind her, and Carrie realized this would not be a quiet event.

She caught glimpses of the ocean through the trees, and understood why her trip would end a mile past Mendocino and not inside the town limits. The seaside community occupied gorgeous geography situated at least two hundred feet above the Pacific on a picturesque cliff. To enter the water from the town would be dramatic but not survivable, so she followed the trail of ribbons to the lower elevation along Route 1.

As she coasted downhill, a splash of purple to her left decorated a rustic sign identifying the Russian Gulch Beach Access. With one last 180-degree turn away from the ocean, she glided along a road sloping to the rocky beach denting the mountainous coastline.

A crowd gathered near a podium created by connecting two picnic tables under a lifeguard stand, but Carrie pedaled past them toward the crashing surf. She manipulated between stones ranging from grenade- to cannon-size, and guided the bike through the hard sand. Dark blue waves crashed on several giant rocks beyond the entrance to the cove, sending white plumes of foam high into the air. A new line of breakers reformed on the rocks' coastal side, creating jagged waves to the beach.

Carrie glanced around the sheltered inlet for evidence of others in the water, relieved by the sight of two kayakers and a few swimmers. She pumped toward the water's edge — thirty feet, twenty feet, ten feet — and the remnants of a fresh wave touched the bicycle's wheels.

After dismounting and throwing her helmet behind her, Carrie stepped into the surf. "My God, this water is cold!" she screamed to nobody able to hear her over the ocean's roar.

She raced toward the next wave, which promptly knocked her over. As those watching enjoyed her battle with the surf, she raised herself and looked again out to the ocean. She dove headfirst into the following swell and swam past the line of breakers. Then, raising both fists and laughing, she gauged the trajectory of the advancing wave, catching it perfectly. She body-surfed to the beach, landing a few feet from her bike.

***

In the crowd of people gathered near the lifeguard stand, Hal nudged Maddie. "She isn't the timid girl who began this trip dipping her toes into the Atlantic, is she?"

"No, Hal. Carrie acts like she owns this ocean!"

"A beautiful sight."

***

Carrie lifted herself from the wet sand, and a muscled lifeguard pulled up next to her on an ATV with oversized tires.

"You might need this, Ms. Brinkley," he said, throwing her a clean floral-colored beach towel. "Jump in, and I'll put your bike on the back. Folks are waiting for you at the lifeguard chair. Welcome to Mendocino, by the way."

"Thank you, sir, but what's going on?"

"The mayor is up there with a few reporters, including one from the TV station. We've set up a mini-podium near the lifeguard stand."

"Goodness! I guess we shouldn't keep them waiting. Am I dressed OK? How's my hair and makeup?" she asked with a mischievous gleam in her eye.

"Perfect for Mendocino, ma'am. Just perfect."

As the ATV approached the chair, Carrie saw her mom and dad, barefoot in the sand and holding shoes in their hands. Russ Dennsion stood beside them, and Carrie covered her mouth, fighting tears.

Russ nodded and motioned his head toward the podium.

She forced intense emotions from her mind and re-focused on the immediate task, whispering to her invisible companion, '*Let's finish this, Howie.*'

Marina Butnari sat on her bike near the back of the crowd and winked at Carrie as their eyes met. Next to her stood Special Agent Hill, looking uncomfortable in a blue suit jacket, his black leather shoes now half-buried in the sand. Jeff Carroll stood on the lifeguard stand with a young Latino man Carrie presumed was the town's mayor. Organizers for the event had attached portable loudspeakers to the sides of the short tower, and the mayor held a wireless microphone. Carrie got off the ATV, and the crowd assembled before the dais burst into applause.

"Folks," began the mayor, speaking into the microphone, "many of us this summer followed the biking journey of Carrie Brinkley from Virginia Beach to our town, so she needs no formal introduction. But, Carrie, we welcome you to Mendocino!"

The audience clapped, and Carrie acknowledged the mayor with a wave.

"Also with us today is Jeff Carroll, one of the Ottawa Bike & Trail owners. Jeff's company sponsored the last half of Carrie's trip, and I invited him to say a few words before bringing Carrie to our stage. Please give him a warm welcome."

The mayor handed the mic to Jeff and climbed down the platform to stand next to Carrie.

When the applause died, Jeff began speaking. "Thank you, friends, and thank you, Mayor Mendez, for your introduction. To stand before you this afternoon is more than an honor. It's a privilege I won't exploit with a long speech or a marketing pitch for our products.

"Carrie arrived in our Kansas community several weeks ago with a body and a bicycle needing repairs. Our local hospital patched up her body, and my company took care of the bike. My partners and I surveyed Carrie's bicycle, and her dad, Hal Brinkley's sophisticated enhancements impressed us. We requested their help to create a new brand of touring bike featuring accessories Hal had attached to Carrie's, and we offered to sponsor the rest of her trip.

"Carrie has been our partner since then, but she also became our friend. She is a remarkable person on many levels, and I'm proud to introduce her."

In the old days, Jeff's last words would have terrified Carrie. Not anymore.

The mayor assisted her in mounting the ladder's first rungs. At the top, Jeff pulled her to the platform and handed her the mic. He gave her a fist bump before descending the makeshift stage to join the mayor below on the sand.

"Thank you, friends, family, mayor, and citizens of Mendocino. I stand here today, dripping wet with no makeup, still clothed in cycling shorts and a jersey, with shoes that now squish when I walk — after my first swim in the Pacific Ocean. It was amazing — and cold!"

The audience cheered, and Carrie waited several moments to continue.

"I'm honored by your enthusiasm and appreciate your hospitality in allowing me to speak. Cyclists cross the country yearly, and, in contests, the fastest of them finish the trip in less than two weeks. Mine took two months. I didn't make the journey to win a prize, though, and I'm not a professional biker. I did it to see if I could."

Carrie paused, glancing at her parents and Russ for a few seconds. "And during the incredible adventure, I found out things. I discovered I *couldn't* do this — not by myself. I needed help — lots of it, which I received from so many people in so many places. Sometimes the support came without asking, from people I had never met. At other times, behind the scenes, nameless professionals in our government who I'll never meet kept me safe. With these crucially important collaborations, I only had to keep the bicycle pointed west... and pedal.

"Many in our nation, no doubt including some of you gathered here, face more serious challenges in this trying year than completing a cross-country bicycle trip. The hurdles I faced during my journey pale by comparison or in importance to yours. But I learned — *witnessed* — that collectively, we have the resources to prevail over anything. We may disagree on politics, religion, sports teams, and which social media platforms perform best, but we agree on the more important things. Everywhere I went, I experienced your willingness to help, your heart, your pride in the place you live, and your love for family. These traits solidify us as Americans and make us great. You helped me finish my epic expedition, and we'll help each other through the pandemic. My experience this summer gave me insight into other things I can do in life, as well as improved skills to do them, and I'll start applying those tomorrow. Thank you."

When she reached the sand from the ladder, the mayor half-laughed and asked, "Are you planning to run for my job, or the governors?"

"Neither, Mayor. My two-month vacation ends today, and it's time for me to get back to work."

"Well, you made a nice start. We appreciate that you chose our community to end your remarkable odyssey. I believe our local TV reporter would like to speak to you, but call me if I can do anything to accommodate you during your stay."

Carrie concluded the requisite interviews and found her parents standing next to Russ. "Dad, you hate the beach! What on earth are you doing here?"

"No way I'd miss this! I'm... *we're* so proud of you, Carrie!"

"Thanks, Dad. I found out some things about myself this summer that will help me for the rest of my life. I'm glad I got the opportunity to make the trip. I know I've worried you and Mom, but thank you for supporting my decision. How long will you stay in Mendocino?"

"We fly back to Norfolk tomorrow. Flights are inexpensive because of the pandemic, and only half the seats were taken on the way here. We could purchase a seat for you on the same flight going back."

Carrie glanced at Russ. "Thanks, Dad, but I'm going to stay here for a couple of days with my friend Marina. That's her walking this way. We already booked a room at the Headlands Bed & Breakfast in town."

As Marina reached the group, Carrie said, "Marina, meet my parents, Hal and Maddie Brinkley, and this is Russ Dennison."

"What a pleasure," said Marina. "The past week biking with Carrie was a thrill, and I doubt you'll be surprised that she told me much about each of you."

"Oh, Marina," said Maddie. "Carrie called us from Reno, and her tale horrified Hal and me. Thank you so much for keeping her safe!"

"You're welcome, ma'am, but I only took care of her for about thirty minutes outside Austin. Since Reno, she's taken care of me. The man standing by the podium has protected your daughter since Colorado. Can I introduce you to Special Agent Douglas Hill?"

"Oh, my goodness," said Maddie. "Of course! Can you and he join us for dinner tonight? Russ Dennison plans to come, too."

Marina focused on Carrie as she replied. "No, sorry, we can't make that because Special Agent Hill and I need to return to Reno for a meeting at our field office first thing tomorrow morning. I'm afraid, Carrie, I can't stay here with you as we planned, either."

Carrie registered the quick wink from Marina. "Mom and Dad, let me speak with my friend before she takes you to meet Special Agent Hill."

Turning toward Marina, Carrie whispered, "What's going on, and when did Doug get here?"

"He flew to Reno last night and drove four hours this morning for this ceremony. It works out for me because he can take my bike and me back now. Based on the evidence Sloan provided, the District Attorney in Norfolk charged Silky and Damien Brown with the murder of Teresa Dill, and all three prisoners will transfer to Virginia to await trial. Doug and I will meet tomorrow to discuss his next assignment with the Bureau. I perceive you might have a little work to do with Russ, so why don't I take your parents to meet Doug and leave you two alone for a few moments?"

"Oh... wow. Of course. I understand. Thank you," Carrie stuttered. "I'm shocked, and happy, to see Russ. I'm not sure where we stand, though. A quick word with him, away from my parents, might not be a bad idea. I love you, Marina, and can't wait to do this again sometime."

"I'm holding you to that. Get going."

Marina led Hal and Maddie through the sand to meet Special Agent Hill, and Carrie turned to Russ. "You surprised me, Russ... and I'm glad you're here, but—"

He stopped her with a hug, and neither spoke as they embraced. Russ finally pulled away. "I overreacted when we last spoke on the phone, and I'm sorry. We have some things to work on, but we should discuss those together."

"I agree. When can we start?"

"Well, I took off for a few days. Could you use some company here in Mendocino?"

"Are you kidding me? Absolutely! The roommate I expected just bailed to go back to Reno!"

"Does your room at the Headlands have an extra bed?"

"Nope. Only the one."

"Good!"

An older gentleman approached Carrie and Russ as they maneuvered Carrie's bike toward Russ's rental car. White-haired and polite, the man said, "I don't want to delay you two, Carrie, and I'm aware you've had a long and busy day. I hope you'll accept my card and call me when your schedule allows. My name is Edgar, and I'm a writer. I believe your adventure across the United States might have popular appeal, and I would like to write the story. Call or email me if you have an interest, and enjoy Mendocino!"

Carrie thanked the man and examined the card:

E. A. Coe
Stories With Heart
www.eacoe.online

THE END

ACKNOWLEDGEMENTS

Thanks to all who helped me with *Pedaling West*, in small ways and large. When I engaged in writing after a long business career, among my most valued learning tools were the blogs offered by Lane Diamond (AKA Dave Lane) on his company's website. This year I was fortunate to have my manuscript accepted by Lane's company, Evolved Publishing, and Mr. Diamond edited the book. I doubt there are better, or more meticulous, editors in the world, and I'm appreciative of his help. Evolved Publishing artist, Kris Norris, created the stunning cover.

Beyond the significant efforts of these professionals, many others contributed to the book. Thank you to my bicycling enthusiast in-laws, Steve and Judy, and my good friend, Don, for their invaluable input relating to long-distance biking, and to the members of my writing group, Jim and Elizabeth, for their generous early editing and feedback. Over thirty fans reviewed early drafts of the story, many providing input affecting it positively. Thank you, Vicky, Philip, Candy, and Michael.

And, of course, thank you to my longest-standing partner, best friend for over fifty years, and wife, Jean. The new writing career would be no fun at all without your daily participation.

ABOUT THE AUTHOR

E. A. Coe... is F. Coe Sherrard, a former United States Naval aviator and career business executive. A graduate of Western Maryland College (now called McDaniel College), Coe is the award-winning author of three other novels, as of January 2023: *Full Count*, *The Road Not Taken*, and *The Other Side of Good*. Married to Jean since 1971, Coe has three children and six grandchildren, and lives in Edinburg, Virginia.

For more, please visit E. A. Coe online at:
Website: https://eacoe.online/
Goodreads: www.goodreads.com/author/show/20327313.E_A_Coe
Facebook: www.facebook.com/AuthorEACoe
Instagram: @EACoe2
Twitter: @EACoe2
LinkedIn: www.linkedin.com/in/FCSherrard/

WHAT'S NEXT?

During a magical evening made possible by a high school reunion, Tyrell Harrell and Siena Tyson discover that romance can endure a decade-long dormancy.

THE ROAD NOT TAKEN
(This newly revised and edited Second Edition will be releasing in September 2023.)

Can Tyrell and Siena's rekindled relationship now survive the challenges of military combat and small-town politics? Ty is a United States Marine Corps pilot, and his job takes him to faraway and dangerous places; Siena owns a small bookkeeping practice in the same town the couple grew up in, and her history there makes life complicated.

They don't give in and never give up, but will that be enough? Life's path is unpredictable, and success is never a certainty. While they courageously push forward addressing the calamities in their way, Ty and Siena get help from heroes who come from unsuspected places.

More from Evolved Publishing

We offer great books across multiple genres, featuring high-quality editing (which we believe is second-to-none) and fantastic covers.

As a hybrid small press, your support as loyal readers is so important to us, and we have strived, with tireless dedication and sheer determination, to deliver on the promise of our motto:
QUALITY IS PRIORITY #1!

Please check out all of our great books, which you can find at this link:
www.EvolvedPub.com/Catalog/

Thank you!

CPSIA information can be obtained
at www.ICGtesting.com
Printed in the USA
BVHW041826030423
661672BV00007BA/537